MW00901066

The Skipper's Captain

By C.S. CROOK

Copyright © 2014 by Carolyn Sue Crook

The right of Carolyn Sue Crook to be identified as the Author of Work has been asserted by her in accordance with the Copyright, Designs and Patents Act 1988.

All rights reserved, no part of this publication may be reproduced, stored in a retrieval system, or transmitted in any form or by any means, electronic, mechanical, photocopying, recording, or otherwise, without prior written permission of the Author. This book may not be lent, resold, hired out or otherwise disposed of by way of trade in any form of binding or cover other than in which it is published, without the prior written consent of the Author.

This book is a work of fiction. Names, characters, businesses, places, events and incidents are either the products of the author's imagination or are used in a fictitious manner. Any resemblance to actual persons, living or dead, events or locales is entirely coincidental.

Carolyn Sue Crook. The Skipper's Captain

This is a heartwarming nature series about a little boy who longs for a dog of his own and an elderly man who is forced to give up his beloved pet. Johnny moves from the desert of West Texas to the West Coast fishing village, Fort Bragg, California, and has to leave behind dear friends and his only pet a horned toad. Just up the road from Johnny's new home, he discovers a scary looking dilapidated old house. There he finds an elderly, grumpy man who has a dog named Trouble. The man tries to scare Johnny away, but Johnny does not scare easily. Later, in 'The Heroic Dog and Boy', Johnny goes back to visit the elderly man and realizes that something is very wrong. The man's dog is straining against its chain and barking wildly at the house. Later, in 'The Magic Wishbone', Hazel, one of Johnny's new friends, makes a wish for the first time ever on Thanksgiving Day, with her mother using a magic wishbone. She refuses to say what she wished for and insists that the magic needs time to happen, although she doesn't understand exactly how magic works. In 'Johnny's Treasure Adventure', Johnny and his friends help to solve a mystery which spans beyond a century, when they find buried treasure near the beach. Together, with the help of the police department, they find answers for how the treasure wound up where it did and who it belonged to. But there is one piece of jewelry in the treasure chest that turns out to have a ghost attached to it. The ghost makes it frighteningly clear that no one else is to have the ruby necklace. This series is about friendships and difficult decisions. It is also about family and how hard it is to move away from dear friends. Step into Johnny's world and follow him on his adventures where the wildlife and scenery comes vividly alive. This series is packed with action and drama, but most of all, it about people caring about and for one another. In this series you will find horned toads, rattlesnakes, raccoons, birds, ponies, fish and a slug, which are all a good mix for children with inquisitive minds.

There are six books in 'Johnny's Adventure' series; #1 'Johnny's Reptile Adventure', #2 'The Skipper's Captain', #3 'The Heroic Dog and Boy', #4 'Finding A Home', #5 'The Magic Wishbone', and #6 'Johnny's Treasure Adventure'.

Contents

Chapter 1

Bright and early the next morning, they continued their journey. Johnny was overjoyed when he finally saw a sign that read, Fort Bragg 33 miles.

His mother, Lilly, made a left hand turn off CA 101 onto Highway 20. After driving about 5 miles on Highway 20, the curves on the highway became sharper and the cliff to the right of them dropped off dramatically. The banks on the left side, however, looked like a lush vertical garden, dappled with long leafed ferns and young slender tree saplings. At one point, Johnny looked out of his window and said, "Mommy, are those tree tops?"

"What?" Lilly asked, because she was focusing so intently upon the roadway.

"Those trees way down in the canyon. Their tops are way up here and I can't see their bottoms."

"Wait until I can find a turn off. This road looks like it was made by a sidewinder." She finally found a slim patch of gravel upon the shoulder of the road and pulled over.

"See," Johnny said, pointing a slim finger at the great expanse of the canyon that lay below them.

"Wow," Lilly said, "that is what Grandpa talked about."

"What?" Johnny demanded to know.

"The stories he told us about the giant trees. They really are giants. I thought he was just embellishing the story for you and the other children," Lilly spoke softly, as if in a trance.

"Yes, now I remember Grandpa talking about giant trees. Are there any other giants?" Johnny asked worriedly.

Lilly turned and looked at Johnny; then she smiled and said, "No, you silly goose. Grandpa said that these trees are called Redwoods, and that they are famous the world over for being the largest trees in the whole world."

"Wow, even sitting here I still can't see the bottoms of the trees," Johnny said in amazement.

"Aren't they beautiful?" Lilly asked him.

Johnny could hear amazement and wonder in his mother's voice and replied, "I think they are. It looks so different here and it's cold."

Lilly reached down, turned up the heater in the car and said, "Yes, isn't it wonderful? It's still summer and it's cool. I can hardly wait until we can see the ocean. My whole life I have never seen one."

"Me neither."

Lilly laughed, reached over and roughed up Johnny's hair affectionately. She checked for traffic and swung the old Ford back out onto the highway, heading westbound once again.

Lilly caught a glimpse of the scenery when she dared. After awhile Lilly said, "I think we could both use a break, what do you think?" Johnny simply looked at her and gave her a small nod. "I will find a nice place to pull over and what do you say we have some lunch. We can share one of those orange soda pops that I bought at the last gas station?"

Johnny's face brightened. "Do you think that maybe after we eat we could take a small hike? We could stretch our legs for a spell."

Lilly looked up at the sky, trying to get a sense of how much daylight they still had left. "I think that will be fine, but just a short hike, okay?"

"That will be just fine," Johnny said.

They found a very scenic turnout on the left side of the road. It was fairly flat, given the rest of the terrain. A small brook meandered between the cleft where two mountains met. There were large boulders scattered about, with some in the brook, splitting it into two small rivulets where the water rushed around them, becoming slim rapids at those points. Some of the boulders were covered with a lime-green moss. Lilly approached one of the boulders with the moss and touched it delicately, not knowing what to expect. It felt soft and plush. The boulder sat right beside the brook. "Do you want to sit here and have our lunch? We can put our feet in the water while we eat."

"Sure, this looks like a good spot," Johnny said, as he picked up some small stones and tossed them one by one into the brook downstream.

"Here, Johnny, would you hold our lunch bag while I climb up onto this rock and then, when I get settled hand it to me please?"

He took the bag, handed it to his mother when she was settled, and then climbed up beside her. Johnny looked all around him. He watched his mother slide her slippers off her feet and dip her toes into the water. Johnny laughed out loud when she squealed and jerked them right back out.

She looked at him and joined his laughter. "That water is freezing!" she said, clinching her toes with her hands. She felt like a young girl again, giggling and sitting there beside the brook. It felt good to her.

Johnny opened the bag and handed his mother a sandwich, and then took one for himself and sat it in his lap. He took out the soda, popped the cap off and took a nice long drink, smiled and handed it to his mother. She took a small sip and handed it back. They ate their sandwiches and admired their beautiful surroundings. A blue jay swooped down from out of one of the redwood trees and flew from one boulder to the next squawking loudly, demanding to be invited to lunch. Johnny pinched off a piece of his bread and tossed it to the bird. The blue jay flew at it with the precision of King at dinner time. That thought made Johnny smile and feel sad at the same time. He missed home already. He looked all around himself again and felt like he was in a different world. The bird swallowed the offering and stared at them with its piercing, beady eyes. It hopped about and squawked, so Lilly tossed him a larger piece. He gobbled it up in just a few pecks and jumped to a rock closer to them, closing in on a free lunch. Lilly laughed and said "What a glutton that bird is!"

It felt good to Johnny to hear his mother laugh so many times in one day. So, maybe, he thought, this change was going to be alright. "Can we hike up there along the water?" Johnny asked Lilly.

Lilly looked up the brook where the mountains joined. "Sure, I don't see why not. If we follow the water, we will not get lost."

"That sounds like a good plan to me," Johnny said, and he placed his trash back into the sack and climbed down off the rock. Lilly handed the sack down to him, climbed back down barefooted and put her slippers back on at the base of the boulder. "Let me just place this back into the car," she said. Johnny nodded and looked for some flat stones to skip across the water. They seemed to be in short supply, but he managed to find a couple and entertained himself until his mother returned from the car. Together, they walked single-file up the brook. The blue jay followed, flying from tree top to tree top, loudly warning his fellow forest mates of the intruders. The tides of his affection seemed to turn, now that Johnny and Lilly were no longer offering him tidbits from their lunch.

There was a slim trail that ran alongside the meandering brook, no doubt made by thirsty wildlife, Johnny thought. Or, perhaps other pioneers like themselves, lured by the beauty of the forest like it was a living enchantress enticing them, drawing them deeper and deeper into the forest, seducing them with its calm and beauty. They rounded a small bend and were amazed a bed of wild irises lay before them. The flowers were small, but otherwise perfect. "Look, Johnny, at those flowers. I had no idea that they grew wild anywhere." Johnny looked at them with the disinterest of any 6-year-old boy.

"Aren't they just the prettiest things that you have ever seen?" Lilly said.

"No," he answered honestly. Lilly looked at him, first in surprise, and then burst out with laughter. Together, they walked on until

4

they found an area where the brook widened considerably, to the point that it was a large pool. This was quite unexpected, but the setting was lovely and serene, with the exception of an occasional outburst from the blue jay overhead.

Johnny walked to the edge of the pool and stared down into the crystal clear water and Lilly quickly flanked him. "Johnny, be careful, don't get too close to the edge," she said breathlessly, for neither one of them could swim. Together, they looked into the aquatic world that lay at their feet. Steelhead trout went about their lives, foraging for whatever nature's bounty was serving up to them on that particular day. Minnows appeared to be on the menu that day.

"Wow, will you look at the size of those beauties!" Johnny exclaimed. "I wish that James and Robert were here to see these, because when we write to them about what whoppers these fish are, they will never believe me."

"Of course they will believe you. They have no reason not to."

He looked up at his mother and smiled. His eyes were sparkling. "Well, when they come to see us, this is the fishing hole that I'm bringing them to."

"I know that they would like that," Lilly assured him, as she placed her arm across his tiny shoulders and drew him up next to her. In that moment, with just the two of them standing tiny and small beneath the towering giant redwoods, Lilly felt that life was going to be good. "I think we need to head back to the car now, sport. I don't want to have to drive that road in the dark and we certainly want enough light left to see the ocean. What do you say?"

Johnny grinned up at her and said, "I say we had better get going." Together, they turned around, both reluctant because there was still so much to explore, and headed back toward the car.

As they drew closer to Fort Bragg, the redwoods receded and gave way to pine trees and huge bushes of rhododendrons. Lilly said to Johnny, "This is like a wonderland!"

"Look Mommy, those flowers are all different colors. There is a dark pink, a light pink, and look, a red one too."

Lilly noticed that traffic seemed to increase, but only slightly. "Yes," Lilly replied, "and I see some white ones up ahead. Look Johnny, there is a little market up there on the right. Do you need to use the restroom?"

"I sure do."

Lilly smiled and said, "Me too." She rolled the car to a stop in front of the Landmark Grocery. There were little houses scattered along the highway now, all in neat rows, and dirt country lanes led off the highway to destinations unknown to them. Johnny and Lilly got out of the car and walked inside the little store. A small bell tinkled over their heads as they entered.

"Welcome," a warm voice said, coming from the left side of the store, where a middle-aged woman sat on a stool behind a long counter loaded with all kinds of goodies. Johnny's eyes lit up. On top of the counter, sat jars and jars of penny candies and Johnny looked up at his mother, hopefully.

Lilly knew at once what he wanted, without a word being spoken. "Yes, go ahead, but only five of them." He smiled and took his time scouring the vast selection, over and over.

The store proprietor smiled and said, "You folks aren't from around here. Are you just passing through or are you visiting somebody; family members perhaps?"

"No, it's just the two of us. We have come to hopefully put down some roots. That is, if the Lord is willing," Lilly replied.

"Well, welcome to Fort Bragg then. I'm sure that everyone in town is going to be pleased to have you folks. I'm Betty," the lady said, as she extended her hand across the counter to Lilly.

Lilly took her hand gave it a gentle squeeze. "Thank you. I'm Lilly and this is my boy, Johnny," Lilly said.

"Well, Johnny, I can see that you have a sweet tooth?" Betty said.

"Yes, ma'am, I sure do."

"What can I get for you?"

"One red hot, a jaw breaker, a red licorice, and two bubble gums please, ma'am?"

Betty filled his order and placed the candy and gum in a small paper sack.
"There you go, Johnny, enjoy," Betty said, handing him the sack.

Lilly dug through her change purse and extended a nickel to Betty.

Betty held up her hand to ward off the nickel. "No, this is my treat. It is my pleasure."

"That is very kind of you. Thank you," Lilly said. "Johnny, tell the nice lady, 'thank you.'"

"Betty," the store owner said.

"Tell Betty, 'thank you.'"

Johnny gave her a heart melting smile and said, "Thank you, Betty. Mommy, I need to go potty."

"Oh, I'm sorry, I almost forgot," Lilly said.

Betty smiled and said, "It's out the door and around the back to the left."

"Thanks again," Lilly said, and then she led Johnny to the tiny bathroom.

When they returned to the car, Johnny offered the open sack to his mother. "Want one?" he asked her.

"No thank you, you go ahead."

Johnny popped the red hot into his mouth. He relished it as they rode along the now increasingly populated highway. Soon, he moved it over into his cheek while he spoke to his mother. "That is sure a nice lady."

Lilly glimpsed over at him and he looked like a chipmunk with that candy in his cheek. She smiled and said, "Yes, she is."

Lilly drove around a gentle bend on the highway and the skyline seemed to drop downward, turning a darker shade of blue. There was nothing but a vast expanse of blue on the horizon in front of them. Lilly sharply sucked in her breath. She reached over and excitedly squeezed Johnny's knee and wiggled it back and forth. "There it is, Johnny, there it is," she squealed with glee. "The ocean, there it is!"

"But we're not there yet," he said.

"Oh, but we will be soon, very soon now." Highway 20 ended at the intersection of Highway 1. Then, she turned right and came to a bridge with a sign that read "Noyo Bridge." She drove slowly now, not wanting to miss anything. "Look, Johnny, on your side is a little fishing village and a harbor."

"Mommy, look at all the boats!"

Lilly could see fishing vessels pouring into the small harbor from the open sea on her side. There was the jetty and the light house, just as Grandpa had told them in his stories about Fort Bragg. It seemed to her now that he hadn't embellished a thing. It was real, but it was still so magical. "Those are fishing boats. Remember, Grandpa said that whole ocean is filled with fish."

"Wow, can I get a fishing pole?"

"I think we might be able to manage that."

"If not, Grandpa taught me how to make one out of a stick and some string."

"Grandpa said that there are some pretty big fish in the ocean. You might need a real fishing pole."

Johnny leaned back and smiled. He was thinking that this just might be alright, after all.

Chapter 2

Lilly found a little road just after the bridge that wound down into the fishing harbor. She pulled her car into a little dirt lot that was filled with rusty old pickups and speckled with a few cars. Just beyond the lot was a wooden pier, where fishing boats of many different sizes and colors rocked in their berths. Many of them had fishermen milling about upon the decks and the dock. They were unloading their catch of the day, from their coolers into wire baskets.

Johnny and Lilly approached the pier and one of the fisherman looked up from his work. Johnny waved to him and he stopped his work, stood up, and waved back. Johnny and Lilly approached his boat. "Excuse us, sir, but could you tell us where we might find a beach, so that we might enjoy the ocean," Lilly asked. The fisherman pushed his hat back from his forehead and burst out in laughter. Lilly looked at him, perplexed.

When he was finally able to contain his laughter, he said with a huge smile and a twinkle in his blue eyes, "Pardon me, ma'am, I didn't mean to be rude, but you folks aren't from around here are you?"

"No, sir, we are not. Does everyone in this town know everyone else?"

"Well, just about."

Just then, there was a racket that came from the end of the pier. "What is that noise?" Johnny asked.

"Well, I guess you aren't from around here. Have you ever been to the coast before, anywhere?" he asked.

"No, sir, we haven't, neither one of us," Johnny replied.

The fisherman flashed a good-natured smile and said, "Wait right there for just a moment." He rummaged around on his boat for a minute and stepped onto the dock with a bucket in his hand. "Come on follow me."

Johnny fell in alongside of him and peered into the bucket. Inside the bucket, small silver fish were flopping all about, piled on top of one another. "Wow," Johnny said, "that's a lot of fish. What are we going to do with them?"

"Make some new friends," the man answered. Johnny turned around and looked at his mother, who was following a few steps behind them. Lilly simply shrugged her shoulders, in response to his questioning look.

They were walking toward the end of the pier where, once again, they heard the strange racket. As they reached the edge, Johnny rushed forward in excitement. Lilly's heart leapt into her throat and she tried to scream out a warning. She started to break into a run but, just as her panic was peaking, the fisherman lunged forward and grabbed Johnny with his free hand. He calmly turned and smiled at Lilly, still clasping Johnny by the collar of his jacket, and asked her, "Does this belong to you?"

"Mommy, look do you see them?" Johnny asked, pointing his finger excitedly at the creatures down on the rocks at the end of the pier. "What are they?"

"Those are your new friends. They will be anyway, just as soon as you toss them a few of these sardines." He reached into the bucket and handed Johnny a fish by its tail.

Johnny smiled broadly and took the fish from the man's large weather-beaten hand. The fish wiggled frantically, slipped out of Johnny's hand and flopped about his feet. Just as Johnny stooped to pick up the fish, it slipped through the cracks of the pier and returned to the sea below. Johnny, who had disappointment written all over his face, looked up at the fisherman. "That was a lucky one," the man said, "but I have a whole bucket of unlucky ones." He extended the bucket to Johnny, so he could choose his own fish. Johnny's broad smile returned instantly. He selected one and held on tightly, as he looked up at the man. "Well, go on, toss them some.

It is about their dinner time. The thing about them is, as far as they are concerned, it is always time to eat."

Johnny flung the fish to the creatures with all his might. One of them knocked another one off the rock and into the water and caught the fish in mid-air. "What a pig that one is. I'm going to give the next one to that poor little guy in the water!"

Lilly laughed and stepped closer. "Those are sea lions, aren't they?"

The man turned to face her and said, "Seals, actually, but they are in the same family. Sea lions are much larger. You will see those sometimes." He extended the bucket to her.

She smiled and waved it away. "No, thank you."

"Oh, go on, have a little fun," he said. She smiled again and gingerly put her slender hand into the bucket to select a fish. The man noticed that there was no wedding band. A good sign, he thought. Lilly tossed the fish underhanded to the seals.

"Mommy, look those seals catch the fish in the air, just like dogs can," Johnny said, while tossing the fish to them just as fast as they could snap them up.

"That boy of yours could make a fine baseball pitcher someday with an arm like that."

Lilly smiled warmly at him and extended her hand to him. "I'm sorry that we didn't introduce ourselves sooner, I'm Lilly and this is my son Johnny." The man took her extended hand and held it softly. Lilly blushed and gave his hand a little shake and slid her hand out of his. "Um, and what is your name?" she felt awkward asking.

"I'm sorry, Hank, Hank Anderson is my name, and my boat is The Skipper."

"We are pleased to have made your acquaintance, Hank."

"I'm pleased as well, Lilly. Say, are you two planning on settling down here in Fort Bragg?"

"Yes we do. Um, where about would the beach be?" she asked.

"Sure, yeah, you just go back out here and follow this little road around. In a short while, it will turn into a dirt road and it will take you to a parking area over there, near the light house and the jetty. To the right of the jetty is where you will find one of the beaches here. There are many different ones. You know, soon you will be able to see the sunset over the ocean. If you have never seen it before, it is the prettiest thing you will have ever seen," he said to her. Hank wanted to add, the prettiest thing I've ever seen is you, but he knew that would be too forward. Instead he said, "I'd love to show you and Johnny myself, but I've still got my catch that I have to get into the cannery."

"Well, we certainly appreciate the time that you have spent on us, and we won't take up any more of it," she said.

"Oh, no, the pleasure has been all mine," he assured her.

She took Johnny by the shoulder and said, "Come on sport, we are losing day light."

Hank, who just felt like he couldn't let her walk out of his life as quickly as she had walked in, called out after them, "Hey, maybe I could take the two of you out on The Skipper on some Sunday?"

"Wow, Mom, could we go?" Johnny pleaded.

"That would be nice," she called back to him and waved farewell and then the two of them returned to the car in search of the beach. Just as they were walking away, an older teenager wheeled up a large cart and leapt aboard the Skipper. He started to unload the catch into wire baskets and then handed them down to Hank, who was still standing on the pier. Hank piled them onto the cart, all the while watching after Lilly and Johnny, until their car went around the bend out of sight.

Tony, who worked on The Skipper with Hank, smiled down at Hank and said, "I've never seen you look so smitten before."

Still looking at the bend in the road and the settling dust from her car, Hank said, "I think I just met my future wife."

Tony laughed and said, "Yeah, right!"

Johnny and Lilly followed the little road and sure enough, just a little way from the fishing pier, it turned to dirt and they could see the jetty and the light house. There was the parking turnout, just as Hank had described. Lilly rolled the Ford to a stop and said, "Are you ready?" Johnny was already opening the door. Lilly giggled and opened hers as well.

"Last one to the beach is a rotten egg!" he called back to her over his shoulder, as he darted off.

"Johnny, don't get too close to that water!"

"I won't," he called back to her, and then continued forward at full steam.

She ran for a bit, but had to stop and pull off her slippers, because they were rapidly filling up with sand. She ran the rest of the way with one of them in each of her hands. She was breathless when she reached the water's edge, but not Johnny; he was squealing with glee, as he ran from each incoming wave. "Johnny, take off your shoes before they get wet."

"It's too late," he called back, as he stood poised to flee yet another incoming wave.

Lilly rolled her eyes skyward and caught her breath. The quality of the sky was changing right before her eyes.

Johnny ran up to his mother and begged her, "Swing me, Mommy, please swing me,"

Johnny was so full of joy! Lilly took him by his tiny wrist, leaned back and whirled him around her. His legs were airborne and her dress twirled around her thighs, when a man stepped out of a sports car, parked next to her car.

14

He looked down at the beach and smiled at the sight of the mother and child. It brought back fond memories of his childhood. The sun was sinking lower upon the horizon. Whenever he could make time to break away from his work, he would always try to catch the setting sun. It was his solace at times, when God just had other plans for his patients and, try as he might, there was just nothing he could do about that.

Lilly and Johnny were both dizzy by the time she returned his feet to the ground. They both fell together laughing wildly. Lilly looked out over the horizon and saw that it was ablaze with color. "Johnny, look how beautiful the sunset is."

"Mom, look at all those colors!"

"Yes, isn't it wonderful?" Lilly asked him, as she dropped down onto the sand and pulled him down beside her.

He leaned up against her and she pulled him into her arms. Both of them relished the warmth that the other's body generated, for it grew colder as the sun sank lower toward the ocean. The colors upon the horizon intensified and reflected upon the waves that were rolling toward the shore, turning the whitecaps sherbet, orange, and pink.

"Mommy, I think this is one of the best days of my life."

"I think so, too," she said, and then kissed the top of his head.

When nature's spectacular show was over, Lilly sighed and gave Johnny a gentle nudge, and said. "We should get going, to see if we can find the Shoreline Lodge before it gets any later."

"Can we come back here tomorrow, Mommy, and maybe see Hank and feed the seals again? That was so much fun feeding them."

"We will see, Johnny, but Hank will most likely be out on his boat."

"Not if we come when he gets back in."

"He needs to unload his boat when he gets back."

Johnny persisted and said, "We can help him. If we help him that will give us more time to feed the seals. Hank said that he would like to show us the sunset."

Lilly smiled at her persistent little man. "We are just going to have to wait and see what tomorrow brings."

"Oh," Johnny said disappointedly.

When they turned to walk back up to where the car was parked, they saw a sports car leaving the small parking area. Johnny had not been aware that anyone else had shared the sunset with them. The crashing waves must have drowned out the sound of the car's engine. They got into their car and Lilly drove back up the narrow road, leaving the scenic harbor behind. They made a right-hand turn back onto Highway 1 and headed towards town. Just at the edge of town up ahead, Johnny could see a flood of lights and smoke billowing skyward. As they approached, he made out what looked like mountains of giant logs, row after row of them. There were even taller mountains of sawdust and he saw what looked like a feed tube at the top of one such sawdust mountain. The tube was spraying more sawdust into the darkening night sky and the mountain was growing taller. This was the lumber mill that Grandpa had worked at in his youth.

The mill stretched out for quite a ways. It was a huge operation. Johnny saw a sign that pronounced that Highway 1 had turned into Main Street and finally, on the right side of the road, small businesses began to appear. They all looked to be brightly painted and well maintained. There were still a few cars parked in the front of some of the buildings, but for the most part, it looked like the little coastal town was rolling up her sidewalks in preparation for the looming darkness. Johnny thought that it was the dinner hour for most folks and that thought made his stomach growl loudly.

Lilly looked over at him and smiled, "Was that your tummy growling at you?"

"It was. Aren't you hungry too?" Johnny asked.

"Yep, I'm starving. We had lunch a long time ago. Let's see if we can hurry up and find the Shoreline Lodge." Lilly saw a brightly lit Flying A service station up on the right side of Main Street. "I think I'll just pull in here and ask for directions, so not to get us lost." She pulled in next to one of the gas pumps, looked down at the gas gauge and frowned. The needle sat just above the quarter of a tank mark. A tall slender gentleman with a stock of dark wavy hair walked up to her window and grinned from ear to ear at her. She couldn't help but to smile back, for his smile was contagious.

"Fill her up?" he asked in a cheery voice.

"No, I had better not tonight, could you please give me just five dollars' worth of gas?"

"I would be pleased too, ma'am." When the attendant finished pumping her gas, he returned to her window. "Let me get that front windshield for you."

"No, I think it is alright for now. You have been kind enough, but may I trouble you for directions to the Shoreline Lodge?"

"Oh, that's no trouble at all! You just follow Main Street here; clear out to the north of town. And just when you think you're going to wind up in the boondocks, she will be sitting pretty on the seaward side of the road."

Lilly handed him a five dollar bill and said, "Thank you, sir."

He tipped his cap to her and said, "At your service, ma'am, anytime."

She smiled at him and pulled back out onto Main Street, heading north. The businesses that Johnny had seen on the edge of town gave way to store fronts that became way more elaborate. These were once grand Victorian homes that had been converted into small shops. From what he could see, each seemed to specialize in something else. That made for good business neighbors, he was sure. There were more people milling about on the sidewalks and coming in and out of the shops.

It was not very long at all until traffic began to drop off and the lights from all the activity in town started to fade back into the night in the car's side mirrors. It was kind of spooky driving out here on such a dark road in an unfamiliar place, Johnny thought. He felt better when they rounded a bend and saw a sprawling lodge on the left, seaward side of the road. Johnny remembered what the gentleman had told them and he smiled, as his mother slowed the Ford and turned onto the county lane that led to the lodge. She slowly guided her car to the front of the lodge, turned off the engine, rested her head in her arms upon the steering wheel and said a silent prayer; a prayer of both gratitude and hope. Johnny sat in the car beside her and silently looked around. He was trying to get a sense of the place. She finally lifted up her head, took a deep breath and said, "Are you ready?"

Chapter 3

"I think so. I sure hope that they have some good food."

"I hope so too," she said, and then Lilly opened her car door and stepped out into the cold damp breeze that swept in off the ocean. Johnny could hear the waves breaking on the shoreline behind the lodge. Seagulls sat on ropes that ran from iron rings attached to driftwood logs, which were long ago cut into posts. They followed the path that ran between the ropes and the seagulls appeared to be totally unfazed by Johnny and Lilly's presence.

Johnny pulled his unzipped jacket tightly around his little torso. "It is freezing here."

Lilly nodded in wholehearted agreement. Finally, they came to some very large wooden doors. Johnny reached for an antique iron handle; it was ornate with inlaid brass. He closed his fingers around it, braced himself and began to pull. To his amazement the door swung open easily. Straight ahead, at the end of a gigantic dimly lit room, was a blazing and crackling fire, a welcoming sight for both of them. There were wooden tables and high backed chairs in orderly rows throughout a large portion of the room. The ones nearest the fire had dinner guests that were enjoying their food and wine, lost in conversation. The diners seemed to be oblivious to Johnny and Lilly. To the right of the door was a bar with empty stools and behind that was a long window that opened up into the kitchen. He could see a chef busily preparing meals. As Johnny's eyes adjusted to the dimness of the room, he saw that to the left of the door and deep along the wall, there was a bar with a very large mirror that ran along the entire length of the bar. There, the patrons had all turned on their stools and were looking directly at the two of them. A gentleman with a round face, white hair, and a flowing white beard came out from behind the bar, wiping his hands on a long white apron. "Good evening ma'am would you and the young gentleman like a table?"

Lilly looked around her nervously, because she was sure that they could not afford to eat dinner there. She said, "I'm looking for Lou."

The gentleman said, "I'm Lou, how may I help you?"

"I'm Lilly Middleton; I believe that you have a job for me?"

"Yes, I'm happy to welcome you to the Shoreline Lodge. This must be your young man?"

"This is my son, Johnny."

Lou bent down and shook Johnny's hand and said, "I'm glad to meet you, Johnny. Have a seat here at the bar." He gestured toward the long bar, which was made of the most unusual wood that Lilly had ever seen. "Are you thirsty?" he asked them.

"Thirsty and hungry," Johnny said eagerly.

"Johnny mind your manners, we will get something later."

"Mom, I thought you said that...."

"Hush," she told him.

"Nonsense, it is late enough for a young boy. It is my treat." He turned and crossed the room, and then walked through some swinging doors at the end of the bar into the kitchen. Soon, he came back, followed by a young man with curly red hair and red freckles to match. "This is Rudy; he will take care of your order." Rudy gave her and Johnny a small polite bow. The older gentleman then said to Rudy, "Rudy, anything at all on the menu is on me."

"Yes sir, I will personally see to it," Rudy replied.

"Wow," Johnny said, as Rudy handed each of them a menu.

Johnny and Lilly made their selection, with Rudy standing politely nearby. There were many items on the menu that neither of them had ever heard of before. Lilly thought it was best to stick with what they knew. One thing was very clear about the menu; nothing came cheaply, even if it was just an order of fried potatoes.

20

Johnny got a soda and Lilly a glass of water; they were both very thirsty. The moment that their glasses were empty, Rudy had them refilled. Rudy then asked, "What will be your pleasure?"

"I would like the grilled snapper and my son would like to have the spaghetti and meatballs, please."

"Very well, I shall submit your request to the kitchen."

"Thank you," Lilly said.

Rudy had just returned with a huge loaf of freshly baked bread, when Lou sat down upon a barstool next to her. "As I said in my letter to my friend, I will put you and Johnny up, and you can cook for room and board only. If you're any good at cooking, and pull me in a lot of new customers, I'll give you a salary, but only after you have proven yourself."

"Oh, sir, thank you. That is more than fair."

"I would like you to cook the breakfast and lunch shift. My staff will show you the ropes, but there is always room for innovation. The innovation part is what I hope will draw in the new customers. I suspect that you bring a bit of the South with you?"

"It is all that I have ever known."

"Well then, it is fair to say that it will show up in your cooking. We have a few good old boys that miss their momma's cooking in this town."

Lilly smiled and replied, "I'll do my best, sir."

Lou warmly returned her smile and said, "I'm sure that you will. We have some little cabins off to the side of the lodge here, just along the drive that you came up. There are some that are set up with small kitchens. I think one of those will be best for you and your boy. I will put you up in the one at the end, the farthest up the drive. It will afford you some privacy from the guests."

Rudy came through the swinging door with plates covered by silver domes. Johnny had never seen anything like that. Rudy sat the

21

plates down in front of them and removed the domes. Aromatic steam wafted into the air, tantalizing the taste buds of both Johnny and Lilly.

Lou saw Johnny's eyes brighten. Then Lou smiled, stood up and said, "You two enjoy your meal. I will bring you the key so you can get settled, after you have finished."

Johnny fell into his plate that was piled high with spaghetti and meat balls. Johnny ate like a starving man. Lilly looked over at him and he had red sauce all over his mouth and chin. She smiled, leaned over and quietly said, "Johnny, wipe your chin." He started to wipe his mouth with his sleeve. Lilly caught his arm just in the nick of time. "With your napkin," she whispered.

Johnny looked over at her and grinned, sheepishly. He wiped his mouth and took a long drink of his soda. "They sure do have a good cook," he stated, loudly.

Rudy, who was standing nearby polishing the bar glasses, overheard Johnny and said, "The chef will be pleased to hear that."

"Please, give him both our compliments. It is a truly magnificent meal," Lilly said.

Rudy smiled politely and nodded. "Consider it done."

Just as the two of them finished, Rudy was there to remove their dishes. Johnny thought he was like a fine-tuned machine. He was amazed by Rudy's precision.

"May I get the two of you dessert or coffee this evening, ma'am?"

"Lilly, please, just call me Lilly."

"Well then, Lilly, would you like to see the dessert menu?"

Johnny looked at his mother and asked, "Please?"

"You must be stuffed, already," she replied.

"I've got room," he assured her.

"Just coffee for me please, Rudy, and I guess a little something for him would be fine."

"I shall be right back with the menu."

Rudy returned with a cup of coffee, placed it down in front of Lilly and then handed them each a dessert menu. "Here, just in case temptation prevails," he said with a smile. She returned his smile and took the menu. After a bit of studying the menu, she helped Johnny with his selection. Like magic Rudy appeared in front of them, just as they closed the menus. "What you would like?" Rudy asked, with eyebrows raised dramatically.

"He would like the layered chocolate cake."

"Excellent choice," Rudy proclaimed and looked at her quizzically.

"Oh, the coffee's fine for me, thank you."

"One slice of layered chocolate cake is coming right up." Rudy spun on one of his heels and was gone. The cake was sitting in front of Johnny in no time at all. "I took the liberty of bringing the young gentleman a glass of milk," Rudy said, and placed a tall glass of milk down alongside the cake. "It has been my experience that one can't have a huge slice of chocolate cake without the accompaniment of milk."

"You are the greatest!" Johnny exclaimed.

"Thank you, young man."

"You can just call me, Johnny."

"Very well, Johnny, enjoy."

"I sure will," Johnny said, and with his fork cut a big chunk of cake from the slice and stuffed it in his mouth. Lilly couldn't help but giggle at the sight of him. He loaded up his fork again and held it up to her, offering her a bite this time. She leaned over and accepted his unspoken offer.

23

"My word, that is delicious," she said. Johnny shook his head in agreement and then stuffed more cake into his mouth. He offered her another bite. "No, that is enough, but thank you." She couldn't believe it, but he was able to finish the whole thing. "I don't know where you put all that?"

Johnny grinned and rubbed his belly. "I put it right here."

"I hope everything was satisfactory?" Lou said from behind them.

Johnny and Lilly spun around on their bar stools to face him. Johnny was the first to reply, "Yep, it sure was."

"It was lovely, thank you so much," Lilly said.

"Here is your key, I'm sure you folks are exhausted. If you find anything lacking in the cabin, the night clerk can let you into the housekeeping storeroom for anything that you might need, but everything should be in order."

Lilly took the key from his hand and noticed the number seventeen on it. "I want you to know that we are so grateful."

"Don't mention it. Have a restful evening, and I will see you at 8:00 am. After that, your shift will start at 4:00 am. There is a lot of food preparation to get the day started here."

"Yes, sir," Lilly said.

"Goodnight," he said, and walked away.

Johnny and Lilly walked back along the path leading to their car. He noticed that the seagulls were now absent, gone to some protected spot for the night, no doubt.

They both pulled their jackets tighter around them, shivering. "Let's hurry, Momma, I'm freezing," Johnny said, quickening his pace. Lilly followed him to the car. Once they were inside, they found that it was no relief from the damp cold that engulfed everything. Johnny's teeth chattered audibly as Lilly cranked the engine over and backed out of the parking spot. As she did so, her headlights raked over the length of the lodge. It was a grand old place, even in this

24

light. They headed back up the lane until they came to the last cabin in the long string and pulled into the tiny drive in front of it.

They stepped out of the car and walked up onto a little porch. There was a bare light bulb that shined right over the number seventeen. Lilly turned the key in the lock and the door swung open, as if inviting them in. Johnny shook off an eerie feeling; after all, he was bone tired. He felt for a light switch alongside the door frame and found it. He flipped the switch and light flooded the tiny room. He caught his breath. It was a small room, but it was beautiful. There was a small bed on either side, with thick floral bedcovers and matching pillows. Johnny ran into the room and plopped himself down on one of the beds. "Aha, this one is mine."

"Take your shoes off, young man," Lilly said, as she walked past him to the kitchen that lay beyond.

She found another switch and lit up the kitchen. It was modest, but had everything she would need. She walked back into the room with Johnny and saw that he was fast asleep, shoes and all. She sat down at the end of the bed and removed his shoes and slid him in under the covers. She slipped off his coat and laid his head upon the pillow. She then sat down on her own bed and said a silent prayer of gratitude. She looked around and found the little furnace and turned the knob and it rumbled to life. She needed to make another trip out to the car, before turning in for the evening. She summoned the will to go back out into the damp cold. Just one more trip, she told herself, and then I get to crawl under those luxurious blankets.

She went out and rummaged through the trunk of the car for the items that they would need in the short term. She could finish unpacking at the first morning light, before she walked over to see Lou. She stuffed a couple of bags underneath each arm and closed the trunk with one of her elbows. Then, she walked back in and prepared for bed. She laid her head down upon one of the pillows and pulled the covers up tightly under her chin. Lilly soon joined Johnny in a deep, peaceful sleep.

Johnny opened his eyes the following morning. The ceiling of the cabin was the first thing that he saw. He blinked his eyes in

25

confusion, turned over in the bed and faced the center of the room. He saw his mother in the bed across the room from him. Although sluggish at first, his memory of the day before returned. He threw back his covers and leapt onto her bed. "You need to rise and shine, Sunshine!" Lilly opened her eyes, just to thin slits, groaned, closed them again and rolled over facing the wall. Johnny gently shook her shoulders, "Sunshine, you've got to get up!"

Lilly sat up in the bed and yawned, stretching her arms high above her head. As she was lowering her arms, she reached out and grabbed him. He squealed in delight and wiggled to get free. She held onto him and tickled him. He wiggled and kicked his legs, giggling wildly. "I'm going go pee my pants," he squealed. She let go of him and he rolled off the bed onto the floor. "Ha, ha, I tricked you."

She pretended that she was going to spring on top of him. He rolled across the floor until he was beside his bed. She swung her legs over the side of the bed, stood up and stretched again. Johnny leapt to his feet and made ready to dodge her. She laughed and headed for the bathroom instead. She washed her face and called out to him from over the towel, "Are you hungry?"

"I'm always hungry," he called back to her.

"You're on a growth spurt."

"What does that mean?"

She walked back into the room. "It means that you're growing, you silly goose."

"Yep, pretty soon I'm going to be as big as you."

"I think you're going to be taller."

He smiled proudly and asked, "Do you really think so?"

"I do think so." He beamed up at her. She handed him a clean shirt and said, "Now go in there, wash up and put this on. We need to get going."

"It's a good thing that I woke you up, huh?"

26

She shook her head in agreement and said, "Yes it is."

While Johnny washed up and got dressed, Lilly brushed her long blonde hair and twisted it into a knot at the nape of her neck. When they were both ready, they set out side-by-side down the long lane to the lodge. Fog lay like a wispy grey woolen blanket upon the meadow, across from the cabins. The dark green pine trees at the meadows edge afforded a striking contrast. Then, Johnny stared straight ahead and marveled at how differently the lodge looked during the daylight. It boasted an almost haphazard mixture of rustic redwood and driftwood, mixed with detailed gingerbread work of an era long ago gone. A lot of the gingerbread work was layered around a long bank of porthole shaped widows and painted a faded shade of slate blue. Johnny was sure it was meant to represent either the ocean or scales on a fish; he was not sure of which.

Parts of the building were curved, which was highly unusual for a building and unpractical, Johnny thought. But she was as grand as she was unusual. As they approached, Johnny saw that the seagulls were back, but a lot more active this morning.

Chapter 4

As they walked through the gigantic doors, the same warm glowing fire greeted them.

"Good morning, and welcome to the Shoreline Lodge, will you be joining us for breakfast this morning?" A pleasant older lady asked.

"You bet," Johnny promptly responded.

The lady looked a bit aghast, but quickly caught herself and corrected her demeanor.

"Yes, please," Lilly said.

The lady put on her best manufactured smile and led them to a table near the fire. "I hope you will find this table to your liking?"

"Yes, this is lovely. Thank you."

She handed them each a breakfast menu and asked, "May I get you started with some coffee or hot cocoa; or perhaps juice?"

"Hot cocoa, you have hot cocoa?" Johnny asked gleefully.

"Well, yes, as a matter of fact we do. It is a specialty of the house."

"I will have the cocoa!"

"I will have the cocoa, please?" Lilly automatically corrected Johnny.

Their server looked at Lilly and asked, "And for you madam?"

"Coffee will be fine for me, please."

"As you, wish," she said, and retreated into the kitchen.

Johnny and Lilly studied the menus. Johnny could not read very well yet, but he sure liked the way the fancy black letters looked on the paper. Lilly spoke softly across the table and said, "They have waffles here. I think you will like that."

"What are waffles?" Johnny asked her.

"They are like a pancake, but really very different, and it says here that you can have fresh local huckleberries on top."

"What are huckleberries?"

"I don't know, but it sounds good. I think this is what I'm going to have," she replied. "Would you like me to find something else for you?"

"No, I think I will try it also," Johnny said.

When the lady returned and sat their steaming mugs down in front of them, she said, "Be careful they are hot."

"Have you chosen your selection from the menu? Or perhaps you would like more time to enjoy your warm mugs and the fire?"

"We have both decided to have the waffles with the wild huckleberries," Lilly said, and handed her the two menus.

"An excellent choice, you shall not be disappointed." She left them to enjoy their drinks.

Lilly leaned across the table and softly said to Johnny, "Blow on that for just a bit to cool it down."

The lady returned with a large silver serving tray and rested it upon a nearby stand. She then placed a plate of waffles before each of them, with what looked like small blueberries in the center of each. "Here we have warm huckleberry syrup for your waffles," she said, as she set a glass carafe on the table. "As for the grand finale," she said, as she turned back to the tray, "freshly whipped cream." She sat the bowl down directly in front of Johnny and smiled broadly. Her smile was genuine and warm and her eyes twinkled.

Johnny did not disappoint. Lilly thought his eyes were going to bulge right out of their sockets. "Wow, this place is the best!" he exclaimed. An elderly couple at a nearby table turned their heads toward them and smiled.

The lady serving them gave a polite curtsy and said, "Enjoy!" She then retreated to the kitchen.

Lilly scooped up a small spoonful of the huckleberries off her waffle. She was curious about the difference in taste between them and blueberries. To her, they looked like blueberries, only smaller. She slipped the spoon between her lips and bit down. Her mouth came alive with the sensation of flavor, as the berries burst inside her mouth. They were both sweet and tart at the same time. She smiled across the table at Johnny who was watching her intently. She smiled and nodded at him. He picked up the carafe and dribbled syrup over his waffle in a swirl pattern, which started at the center, atop the small mountain of huckleberries. Next, upon the small mountain of huckleberries, he piled a huge mountain of whipped cream. He beamed proudly at her from across the table. She could not help but to giggle. He joined her laughter and it felt so good to them both.

Their server returned with pots of both coffee and cocoa to refill their mugs. "How do you find your breakfast?"

"It is truly wonderful," Lilly said

"It looks like someone certainly enjoyed the whipped cream," she smiled affectionately at Johnny.

"Yes, ma'am, I really did."

"I think whipped cream makes just about everything wonderful, but that's just my opinion," she said to him.

"That's my opinion too!" he said.

She smiled at him again and then asked them both, "Is there anything else that I may get for you?"

"This will be fine. Thank you very much," Lilly replied

The server placed the ticket on the table and said, "I will be happy to take care of this when you are ready."

Lilly flushed with embarrassment and said, "I believe that this is on the house."

"Oh, my apologies, I beg your forgiveness! Of course, you must be the new cook."

"Yes, I'm Lilly and this is my son Johnny."

"I'm Jo Lynn and I'm so pleased to meet you," she said, and extended her hand to Lilly.

Lilly took her hand and said, "The pleasure is mine."

"I'm sure it will be a joy to work with you," Jo Lynn said.

"I'm looking forward to it, thank you," Lilly responded.

Just then, Lou stepped through the swinging doors from the kitchen into the dining room. "Good morning, to you all."

The two women responded alike with a "Good morning, sir."

Johnny looked up at him, gave him a great big smile and said, "Good morning, Lou."

"Johnny, where are your manners? You call him sir."

"No, no, the boy has it right, Lou is just fine," Lou said, and Lilly smiled with relief.

"If you will pardon me, I have duties to attend to," Jo Lynn said.

"It was very pleasant to have made your acquaintance, Jo Lynn," Lilly said.

"Thank you," Jo Lynn replied, and she looked at Lou to be excused.

"Well, since you three have met, I guess I will take it over from here," Lou told Jo Lynn. Jo Lynn gave a small curtsy and left them to talk.

"I hope that you found your accommodations acceptable?"

"They are lovely, sir, thank you," she said. "You are most generous."

"Bah," he said, and smiled at her, "come on, let me introduce you two to the kitchen staff." Johnny and Lilly got up from the table and followed him to the set of swinging doors. Lou held one open for them and stepped aside so they could enter. When Johnny hesitated, Lou said, "Go on in, and don't be afraid."

Johnny looked up at Lilly and she nodded and gave him a gentle nudge forward. He stepped through the doors, followed first by Lilly and then Lou. To Johnny, it was like stepping into another world. The stainless steel and black stoves and ovens glistened, and everything else in the room was dwarfed by them. There were pots even larger then Grandpa's cauldron. The air was fragrant with bacon and sausage and the sweet smell of huckleberry syrup. There was a tall skinny man dressed all in white. He had a funny looking white hat on, which was tall and puffy looking. This made the man look ridiculous, Johnny thought. The man looked over at them and grinned. He then went back to his work of flipping pancakes and eggs, with intense precision. He then grabbed two plates from a tall stack from underneath heat lamps, fanned them out in one hand and then used his other hand to slip the pancakes and eggs onto the plates. He turned to one of the large ovens, opened the door, retrieved three slices of bacon for each plate and piled them on top. With that done, he slide them underneath the heat lamps, next to the stack of plates, and rang a small silver bell. He wiped his hands on his long white apron and turned to face them, grinning once more.

Lou made the introductions. "This is Gus; he is the head cook here on the morning shift. He will be showing you all the ropes and you will be reporting directly to him," Lou then said to Gus, "Gus, this is Johnny and Lilly."

Gus stepped away from his stove and extended his hand first to Lilly. "I'm pleased to meet you," he said.

"I'm very pleased to meet you as well. I look forward to working with you," she replied, and shook his hand.

Gus then squatted down so that he was at Johnny's eye level. He held out his giant hand to Johnny and Johnny timidly clasped a hold of Gus's long fingers. Gus closed his fingers around Johnny's hand and Johnny saw his own hand disappear before his eyes. Johnny instinctively snatched back his hand.

"Johnny!" Lilly exclaimed.

Gus grinned again, stood up, and roughed up Johnny's hair. "That's alright, he'll come around," Gus said confidently. Johnny smoothed his hair back into place with his fingers and shuffled his feet. His eyes darted around the room, as if he was looking for an escape route.

A short and very round woman came around from behind the row of ovens. "This is Molly," Gus said, "she is our prep cook."

"I'm mighty pleased to meet you, miss," Molly said, with a distinct Irish accent. When she saw Johnny, her face brightened and little apple cheeks grew larger on her face as her smile widened. "This is your wee lad?" she asked.

"Yes, this is Johnny."

"He is a mighty fine looking lad, even at such a young age. This boy of yours is going to break a few hearts when he grows up," she said, and winked at Johnny. Johnny looked up at his mother. He was clearly confused.

Lilly looked down at Johnny and said, "She thinks that you are going to be handsome."

"But aren't I already handsome?" All the grown-ups laughed. "Aunty Beth always said I was."

"And she would be right, lad," Molly assured him.

"I will leave you now, to become better acquainted and to go over your duties with the staff," Lou said.

"She will be in fine hands, sir," Molly said.

33

"Of that I am sure, Molly," Lou said, and with a nod of his head to all of them he left the kitchen.

Lilly kneeled down in front of Johnny. "Do you think you can find your way back to the cabin?" she asked him.

"Of course I can, Mommy, it's just right up the road."

"Can you tell it apart from the others, because they kind of all look the same?"

"Mommy, your car is sitting in front of ours."

"You are a very smart boy, Johnny." She removed her watch from her wrist and said to him, "Look here at the face of this watch, Johnny. See this little hand and this big hand? When they both reach the top to this number twelve, you come back here for lunch, alright?" Johnny nodded. "And, Johnny, you have to promise me that you will stay away from the cliffs at the back of this lodge. When I get off work, we will find a safe place to look at the ocean."

"Can we go to the beach again?" he asked eagerly.

"Yes, if you can promise me that you will do as I ask. You may play around the cabin, but stay away from behind the lodge."

"Okay, Mommy, I promise."

"That is very good." She gave him a kiss on the forehead and said, "I will see you here for lunch, when the big hand and the little hand are both on the twelve."

"Alright, Mommy, I will see you at lunch time, but I don't need this watch, because my tummy knows when it is hungry."

"Take the watch, because I will have your lunch ready at that time."

"Okay, okay, I will." He gave the grownups a shy little wave and headed out the big wooden door toward the cabin. One of the seagulls flapped its wings and squawked at Johnny as he walked past them, down the planked walk in front of the lodge. "Don't you have some fish to catch or something?" The seagull just stared at him with its little beady black eyes. "Maybe, at lunch, I can bring you a little crust of bread. Would you like that?" The seagull flapped its wings and squawked again as if it understood. "Alright, I'll see what I can do," Johnny said, and walked up the little country lane that led to the row of cabins.

He saw that a few cars speckled the front drives of a couple of the cabins. The cars were fancy, newer models. He could see some people walking off in the distance. All grownups he thought, disappointedly. He reached his cabin and noticed for the first time that, across the road and just a little of the way up toward the highway, there was a small house. It sat back from the road a bit, mostly hidden by trees. He hadn't noticed it earlier this morning, because of the fog. He was suddenly intrigued that there was something to explore. He walked past his cabin and up the road to have a closer look.

He stopped in front of the little dirt driveway. An old rusty pickup sat at the very end, nudged up next to a dilapidated house. Under a shade tree, Johnny saw a large dog tied to the tree with a chain. It looked at him and wagged its tail. Johnny walked down the little dirt drive and up to the dog. He put out his hand so the dog could sniff it. The dog wagged its tail more vigorously and licked his hand. Johnny petted it on the head and gave its ears a good scratch. Johnny knew that there was nothing dogs liked more than that.

"What on earth do you think you are doing?" a gruff voice spoke, from behind Johnny.

Chapter 5

Johnny jumped a little. He slowly turned around and saw a disheveled-looking, elderly man. "I was just petting your dog, sir."

"Don't you know that dog is vicious?"

"No he's not."

"He is so, he is a German Shepherd. They are bred to rip grown men to shreds. You would just be a snack."

"He's not going to hurt me, he likes me. What is his name?"

"Trouble, it is the same as mine. If anybody messes with either one of us, there is going to be trouble."

"No sir, I would be willing to bet that neither one of your names is Trouble."

The elderly man peered down at Johnny and estimated his age, and he was pretty sure that Johnny couldn't read yet. The man smiled and fished for his wallet in the big pockets of his faded overalls. "Is that so?"

"Yeah, it's so," Johnny said, with newly found confidence. The man opened up a worn and tattered wallet and held it in front of Johnny. "What am I supposed to be looking at?" Johnny asked.

The man thumped a yellowed plastic frame with his index finger, and behind it was a driver's license with a picture of a much younger version of the man that stood before Johnny. "See right here, it says that my last name is Trouble."

Johnny peered closer and saw a name, but since he couldn't read well yet, he simply said, "Oh, I see that you are right."

"Of course, I'm right, what man doesn't know his own name?"

"Well, Mr. Trouble, I sure do like your dog. I hope you wouldn't mind if I come over and pet him sometimes."

"Where did you come from? I haven't seen you around here before."

"My mother and I are from Texas. Are there any other kids around here? I haven't seen one."

"There are, but they live too far for you to go. You will see them when you take the school bus into town."

Johnny's eyes widened with surprise. "I get to ride on a school bus?"

"Yep, you will be taking the bus, unless you were planning on walking into town?"

"No, I think that is great!"

"Is this going to be your first year in school?"

"Yes, I'm going to be 6-years-old real soon. I've been waiting a long time to go to school. What about Trouble?"

"What about him?" The man asked.

"Can I come over here and pet him sometimes? I use to have dogs in Texas, but I had to leave them with my friends. Well, actually, they were their dogs, but we shared them. I really miss them already and my friends too."

"Well, I reckon so, just as long as you are no trouble. We already have enough trouble around here."

Johnny grinned from ear to ear and said, "That will be great and I will be no trouble."

"Where are you folks staying?"

Johnny turned around and pointed through the trees. "Right there, do you see where the blue and white car is? We are neighbors." Johnny beamed at him.

"I can see that," Mr. Thornton said. "Are you visiting the lodge?"

"No, we are living there in that cabin. My mommy is going to be their new cook. She is a really good cook. She is almost as good of a cook as my Aunty Beth."

"Well then, I would like to meet your Aunty Beth."

"You would like her. I miss her too."

"I'm sure I would. Now you had better scoot along. You are tuckering me out with all your chatter."

"I will see you tomorrow, okay?"

"If I'm blessed to see another day, I'll see you tomorrow."

Johnny gave the dog one final pat on the head and said, "Goodbye."

Mr. Thornton stood beside his dog and watched the little man walk down the road. He was amazed at how easily the little guy had walked into his life. He had spent most of his life shutting people out. It wasn't until now that he realized just how lonely he had been all along.

Johnny opened the door to the cabin and dug into his pocket for the watch. He knew that it was not time for lunch yet, because his tummy had not alerted him. He didn't bother to even look at the watch; instead, he placed it on the nightstand beside his bed. It had been bugging him all morning, bouncing around in his pocket every time he took a step. He was just happy to be free of it. He looked around the cabin. It was very nice. A lot nicer than anything he could ever remember living in. The only thing it was missing was other children. He felt strong pangs of homesickness. He had mixed feelings. He was sure that his mother was going to be happier here, because Grandpa and Aunty Beth had said so, and they were always right. They had also said that this would be better for him, but right now he just couldn't see it. It was true that he had made at least one new friend this morning, Mr. Trouble, but he just knew that he needed to find some other kids. Even girls would be alright, if that was all there was. Mr. Trouble had said that some other kids would be on the school bus. Maybe some of them lived closer than Mr. Trouble thought. Bored, Johnny stretched out on the bed, and before he knew it, he was sound asleep. He woke up to the sound of his growling stomach. He picked up the watch and peered at the little oval glass that covered the big and little hands. The little hand was on the twelve and the big hand was almost there as well. He swung his legs over the side of the bed and rubbed the sleep from his eyes. He had no idea he was so tired. He walked out of the cabin, carrying the watch in his hand, and headed for the lodge. The seagulls were off somewhere, probably looking for their own lunch, no doubt, he thought. He also noticed that there were quite a few cars lined up in the parking lot in front of the lodge.

He tugged the large door open and slipped into the lodge. Jo Lynn was there to greet him. "Oh, there you are, and right on time. What a punctual young man."

Johnny had no idea what the word punctual meant, so he just smiled up at her. She led him to the swinging doors and held one open for him so that he could enter. His mother was standing beside Gus at the stove and was wearing the same funny getup as Gus. She was ladling steaming, white soup into small bowls, and placed each one upon saucers that were lined up underneath the heat lamps. She reached up and triumphantly rang the silver bell. She looked over at Johnny and smiled. "Come on, I'll show you where your lunch is," she said to him. He followed her around the bank of ovens. He was surprised at how much space was back here. There were two long wooden tables that were butted up, end-to-end, making a really long table. Here was Molly, working her magic. She had neat piles of all kinds of different vegetables mounded up on one of the tables. She looked up briefly from her work, flashed him a quick smile and then back to work she went, wielding the large chopping knife as skillfully as if she had been born with it in her hand. In the corner was a much smaller table with six chairs. "This is where the staff and any family members take their meals," Lilly said.

Johnny saw that there was a bowl of the same white soup sitting on the table. There was also a smaller bowl filled with little round puffy looking crackers and a tall glass of milk. "What is this?" he asked her.

"That is a cup of clam chowder and oyster crackers. I think you will really like it." She pulled a chair out for him, "Here, go ahead and sit down and get started. I've got to get back to work."

He sat down, looked up at her and sadly asked, "Aren't you going to eat with me, Mommy?"

She leaned over and kissed him on the forehead. "I can't, I have to get back to work. I'll eat my lunch later, but we will have dinner tonight together."

"We'll have dinner, after we go to the beach?" he asked.

"Yes, after we go to the beach," she said, and then she was gone, back around the ovens.

Johnny dipped his spoon into the creamy white soup. He wasn't sure what to expect, but he was pleasantly surprised: it was delicious. He then popped an oyster cracker into his mouth and enjoyed the crisp crunch of it. He looked over at Molly. She was bent over the large table, so focused upon her work that she seemed oblivious to him being there. He finished all of his soup and then downed most of his milk. Now, he thought, since he was well rested and fed, it was time to go exploring. He walked past Molly, who looked up and said, "I'll see you later, lad."

Johnny smiled and nodded. When he rounded the bank of ovens, he waved to his mother and Gus. "I'll be off work at 4:30," she called after him. He nodded and went through the swinging doors. Once he was out of the lodge, he realized that he had forgotten to bring a treat for the seagulls. He shrugged and told himself that he would try to remember them tomorrow.

He knew that the cliffs were off limits, so he headed toward the huge meadow. The grass was long and golden and there was a tall row of trees at the far end. They were not the redwood trees that they had seen on their way into Fort Bragg, but they were still rather large and beautiful. He decided to make the trees his destination, so

40

he set off toward them. He could hear the constant crash of the waves upon the cliffs in the distance. He looked up at the sky and saw the seagulls wheeling overhead, beneath the billowing white clouds. The sky was as blue and pretty as his mother's eyes, Johnny thought.

Suddenly, a flock of funny looking birds flew up out of the grass in front of him. They had one little feather sticking up off their heads. He would ask Mr. Trouble what they were, because Johnny felt certain that he would know. As he drew closer to the trees, he could smell a peculiar aroma, and the closer he got, the stronger the smell became. When he finally got to the base of one of the trees, he looked down at the ground, and all around his feet were these dark brown pods. He bent over, picked one up and sniffed it. It stunk. He looked up at the branches of the trees and could see that they were practically drooping with the weight of the pods. He slipped the pod into one of the pockets of his overalls and was going to ask Mr. Trouble about the stinky trees tomorrow as well. Beyond the trees, he saw a steep incline and thought that he would go have a look. He climbed to the top and then half slid down the sandy embankment on the other side. When he reached the bottom, he saw a huge cement tunnel, which had a little stream running through it. There were wild red and yellow berries growing everywhere along the stream. He reached out, picked one of the red ones and popped it into his mouth. It was much sweeter than the wild huckleberries that he had for breakfast that morning. He picked a yellow berry to taste it. It was okay, but lacked the sweetness of the red berry. He picked one of each and added them to his pocket with the pod from the tree. He would have a lot of questions for Mr. Trouble.

Johnny stepped out onto the other side of the cement tunnel, into a lush valley. It was like he had walked through the tunnel into a different world. There were these big leafy green plants just everywhere, and these beautiful purple flowers. They were the same flowers that his mother had called wild iris, when they had stopped on their way into town. The wild irises were small but very pretty. He would be sure to remember to pick a few for his mother on his way back. Just down the path, Johnny saw huge grassy clumps. They were much taller than he was and they had these giant plumes of what looked like silky feathers. The sound of the ocean grew stronger in this almost magical place. Down the path, a little bit farther, he could make out a wooden plank pathway. He drew closer, as the magic lured him in. He stepped upon the first wooden plank and could see another stream running beneath. There were some beautiful plants up ahead and, as he drew nearer, he had to clamp his fingers over his nose, because they stunk worse than the tree pods. The magic was temporally broken, but only until he saw what lay beyond. He sucked in his breath and a smile lit his face. He pinched his arm, just to make sure that he was not dreaming. A very tall and steep golden embankment stood before him in the distance, and at its top and bottom were giggling children of all different ages. They were clutching huge pieces of cardboard and sliding down the grassy embankment upon them. They squealed with joy each time on their way down. Johnny broke into a run, for he could not contain his excitement.

He ran to the base of the hill and had to jump out of the way of an incoming boy on a cardboard sled. The sled came to a stop and the boy stepped off and stared at Johnny. All the other children stopped their play and stood staring at him as well from the top of the hill. The air that had been filled with the joyous sound of the children's laughter just a moment before was silent. After a long pause, the boy who stood at the bottom of the hill with Johnny asked, "Who are you?"

"I'm Johnny, who are you?"

"I'm Bobby, what are you doing here?"

"I'm exploring. That looks like a lot of fun."

"Yeah, it is. Do you want to try?"

"Yeah, I sure do!"

"I'll share my sled with you today, but next time you will have to bring your own, okay?"

"Sure that will be great."

"Well, come on then, follow me." On their way up the hill, the tall, slim freckle-faced boy asked Johnny, "Why do you talk so funny?"

"I don't talk funny," Johnny replied.

The tall boy simply shrugged his shoulders and let it go. All the children waited for them, until Bobby and Johnny reached the top. "This is Johnny," Bobby announced, to his five other companions. One of the girls stepped forward. Her long red hair fell in loose ringlets about her shoulders. She smiled at him meekly and said, "Hi, I'm Hazel." Johnny nodded at her. Johnny didn't pay much mind to girls yet, but this one was very pretty. She blushed and stepped back into the little crowd that had gathered.

A tall older boy, that Johnny guessed was about ten years old, stepped forward next. He held out his hand to Johnny and said, "I'm Fred. I'm Bobby's big brother, and I'm pleased to meet you, Johnny."

Johnny took Fred's hand, shook it and said, "And I'm pleased to meet you."

Next, a blonde girl stepped forward pulling a boy about her own age with her. Johnny noted that the boy allowed himself to be dragged along, reluctantly. "Hi," she said boldly, "I'm Leslie and this is Lester, my bother. We are identical twins, except I'm a girl and he is a boy."

"I can see that," Johnny replied. "I'm glad to meet both of you."

"And we are glad to meet you," she said, doing all the talking for both of them.

The last girl looked to be about a year older than Johnny and she stood to the back of the crowd. She peeked around the others at him. Johnny looked at her and then at Bobby. Bobby said, "That's Donna, she is shy, but only until she gets to know you."

"Yeah," Fred said, "but watch out, once she gets to know you, she'll talk your head off."

Johnny chuckled and waved. "Hi, Donna," he called to her. She quickly ducked behind the others.

Lester whispered something into Leslie's ear and she nodded. She looked directly at Johnny and said, "My brother Lester and I would both like to know why you talk funny?"

Johnny looked at her perplexed. Fred came to his aid. "It's because you are not from around here, are you Johnny?"

"No, but I am now. I live at the lodge. My mommy is a cook there."

"Where did you live before you came here?" Hazel asked softly, encouraging him.

"I lived in Texas."

"Come on," Bobby said, "we'll ride this down the hill doubled-up. You sit up here in the front."

Johnny sat down on the cardboard and Bobby sat down behind him. "Okay," Bobby said, "now we push off with our hands on the count of three. Got it?"

"I've got it," Johnny said, smiling with gleeful anticipation.

Bobby counted, "One, two, three, go!"

Before Johnny knew it they were speeding down the hill with amazing speed. It was frightening and thrilling, all at the same time. He was sure that they would wreck, but instead the sled slowed to a gradual stop when the base of the hill tapered off to level terrain. "Wow that was the best!" Johnny exclaimed.

"Want to do it again?" Bobby asked.

"I want to do it one hundred times," Johnny said, springing up off the sled.

"Well then, come on and grab the other side and let's go!" Together, the two boys lugged the sled up the hill, while the other children took turns riding theirs down the grassy slope.

"This is the most fun I've had in a long time," Johnny confided in Bobby.

"We come here just about every day or so in the summertime."

"Are you going to be riding the school bus?" Johnny asked.

"Yeah, I always ride it, how about you?"

"Yeah, I suppose so. I don't want to have to walk all the way to town."

"What grade are you going to be in, Johnny?"

"I'm going to be in first grade. I've never been to school before. I can hardly wait. All the grownups tell me it is going to be fun."

Bobby shrugged, "Sometimes it is, I think, but mostly recess is the fun part."

"What is recess?"

"It's when the teachers let us go outside to play, except when it is raining, and then we play in the classroom."

"Are you going to be in first grade?" Johnny asked.

"Nope, this year I'm going to be in second."

They had reached the top and waited in line for their turn to ride down the hill again. Johnny watched as Hazel went flying down the hill on her cardboard sled. Her long red ringlets were bouncing all about in the air behind her head. Her laughter drifted up the hill toward everyone who stood at the top. Johnny smiled when she reached the bottom and pretended to tumble off the sled, flinging her arms out dramatically and shrieking.

Bobby looked at Johnny and rolled his eyes. He said one word, "Girls."

Johnny nodded his head knowingly in kinship. "You can sure say that again!" But he thought to himself that this particular girl was different from any he had ever met. He couldn't exactly figure out why. It was just a weird feeling that he had, from the moment he first saw her.

Finally it was their turn. "I'll go in the front this time," Bobby said. "We'll have the same rules as before." Bobby sat down and Johnny sat down behind him. Then, Bobby said, "Okay, on the count of three."

"On the count of three," Johnny said.

Bobby began the count, "One, two, three and blast off!"

At 4:30 p.m., Lilly finished her shift and walked up the lane towards her cabin. There was a soft breeze coming off the water and it felt delightful to her. A small wisp of her hair escaped her hair net and tickled the sides of her face. She brushed it back, but it was to no avail. A pair of chipmunks chased each other across the road up ahead of her. She smiled. Grandpa was right when he said he knew that she would love this place. Even with the curl of the smile still upon her lips, she felt the sting of tears in her eyes. She missed her friends so much, even though she knew that she was making new ones, just this day. Still, she knew that Grandpa, Beth, Buddy and their boys were really more like family, and she was old enough to know that you didn't find that quality of friendship very often in a lifetime.

She turned off the lane and stepped into the little yard in front of her cabin. There was no sign of Johnny, so she thought he must be inside. She opened the door and a smile lit her face with the anticipation of seeing her little boy. The smile faded very quickly, for he was nowhere to be seen. "Johnny?" she called. Her brows furrowed with worry and she stepped back upon the little porch and called his name again. Still there was no response. She felt panic rising in her chest and she struggled to keep it at bay. She raised her hands to her face and cupped them around her mouth. "Johnny?" she called again, and still there was no response. She clasped her hands upon her chest and frantically looked around her. She felt like bolting off in blind panic to search for him, but she wasn't sure which direction to run. She stood, planted upon the porch, frozen momentarily with fear. Her eyes darted up the lane toward the highway. She instinctively ruled that direction out. She looked at the meadow, which stood along the one side of the lane across from the cabins, and could see that it stretched between the cliffs and the woodland. Because of the fog that morning, she had no idea that it went such a large distance. She knew that, in the past, Johnny had never wandered far and she prayed that was the case now. She could not bear to think of the cliffs behind the lodge, so she set out headed toward the meadow. There was a small trail through the grass, made by visiting lodge guests and whatever else that roamed the meadows. Lilly stepped onto the trail and followed it until the trail forked. In one direction, it went toward the cliffs and in the other, toward the woods. She headed toward the trees and again cupped her hands to her mouth and called his name. Nothing but silence came from the woods and the sound of crashing waves came from behind her. Her heart sank and she turned back toward the lodge, for she knew that she needed help, because it would be dark soon. She broke into a run and from behind her she heard, "Mommy?" She wheeled around and ran toward the woods. Tears were streaming down her face and through the blur of tears, she saw her little Johnny emerging from the woods. She ran to Johnny and collapsed to her knees before him. Scooping him up into her arms, she buried her face into the crook of his neck and sobbed so hard that her shoulders shook.

"Mommy, what is wrong?"

"I thought that I had lost you," she sobbed.

"You didn't lose me. I was never lost, Mommy." He patted her on the back and added, "It's okay, Mommy, I'm right here."

She loosened her grip of him and pulled back, wiping at her tears with the back of a hand. She smiled at him, feeling a bit foolish and then she reached out and took one of his shoulders in each hand. "Johnny," she said sternly, "you must promise me; you have to promise me that you will never, ever, go near those cliffs. They are very dangerous."

He looked at her and then over her shoulders in the direction of the cliffs. After a moment, his eyes rested upon her tear streaked face and he asked her, "Did you think I was lost over the cliffs, Mommy?"

"I was terrified that you were lost over the cliffs."

"I promise, Mommy, that I won't go near the cliffs."

She wrapped her arms around him and pulled him close in a warm and loving embrace. Then she whispered into his ear, "Are you ready to go to the beach?"

Johnny wiggled out of her arms and smiled broadly, "I sure am."

Lilly stood up, took him by the hand and said, "Then let's go."

Hand in hand, they walked together to the old blue and white Ford. Lilly opened the passenger door for Johnny and he jumped in. She closed the door, walked to her side, slid in behind the steering wheel and started the engine. "Do you want to go and try to find another beach? I've heard that there are many different ones."

"No, I want to go back down to the same one. I was thinking that maybe we could see Hank again."

She glanced over at him and smiled, "Oh, you were thinking that were you?"

"Yeah I like him, Mommy, he is nice. Don't you like him?"

"Yes, I think he is a nice man too." Lilly turned off Highway 1, onto the little road that led down to the harbor. On their way down to the harbor, Johnny told Lilly all about the children that he had met that day. He told her about the grassy hill and the sleds. He left out the part of him feeling peculiar about Hazel, only because he was confused about it.

When they drove past the docks, Johnny said with disappointment in his voice, "Hank's boat is not here."

"Well, he must still be out fishing. Anyway, he has a job to do. We don't want to make a pest of ourselves."

When they pulled up to the little dirt parking lot, Johnny's mood brightened. He flung open his car door and dashed off toward the beach. Laughing, Lilly got out of the car, walked around to the passenger side and closed his door. When she reached the sand, she removed her slippers and ran toward the shoreline. She saw Johnny plop down upon the sand to remove his shoes. Johnny had just finished taking off his shoes when she reached him. She dropped her shoes beside him and pulled him to his feet. Together, they raced into the waves and their laughter rang out above the pounding of the surf. They ran from the incoming waves, then turned and boldly chased the receding waves back into the ocean. Johnny and Lilly frolicked upon the beach until, breathless, Lilly collapsed upon the sand, but Johnny still played on. She watched him splash in the waves, while the seagulls swooped about all around the two of them.

The sun was dipping lower upon the horizon, when Lilly saw the first fishing boat making its way toward the harbor from the open waters of the sea. It was not very long before she spied another fishing vessel following it and then another was like a large dot upon the horizon. "Johnny?" she called, above the crashing of the surf. He turned to look at her. "It looks like the fishing boats are coming back in. Do you want to go over to the lighthouse on the jetty to watch them come in?"

He flashed a huge smile at her and ran up to where she was sitting. He plopped down beside her, began pulling on his socks and said, "Do you think we will see Hank's boat?"

"I don't know. It depends on when he is coming back in," Lilly said.

Johnny tugged on his shoes and bounced to his feet. "Come on," he said, and extended his hand to her. She took it and he helped Lilly to her feet. She brushed the sand from her backside as they headed off in the direction of the jetty and the lighthouse.

The sun continued to sink lower upon the horizon and by the time they reached the lighthouse, there was a parade of fishing vessels coming into the straight, leading past the jetty and into the harbor. Seagulls darted in and out among the boats, as if they were the escorts of the vessels. Only there was no order amongst the seagulls, so they called out to each other loudly in the fray. The boats heading into the harbor were all different sizes and colors. Each one of them had their own unique name. There was The Jellyfish, The Sea Scout, The Mermaid, and on and on, but The Skipper was not among the vessels in the straight. The water in the strait was much deeper than the water on the beach so, instead of rolling in waves, it sloshed upon the boulders of the jetty. There were large pieces of seaweed caught up between the boulders. It laid there, still wet and shiny in the fading light of the harbor.

"Where is The Skipper?" Johnny asked his mother.

Lilly looked out to sea, just beyond the light house and pointed, "There she is."

Johnny's face brightened, "Where?" he asked.

"See the fourth boat back from the end of the jetty here."

"I see it! I see it!" He shouted with joy and began to wave wildly.

Lilly laughed, "He can't see you yet, Johnny."

Johnny stopped waving momentarily and looked up at her, "Huh?"

"He can't see you yet, because he is too far away."

Johnny watched The Skipper's approach and when she drew near enough, Johnny started to wave again. "They can see me now, can't they Mommy?"

"Yes, I think so," she said. As if to answer his question, The Skipper sounded her horn.

Johnny jumped up and down with joy, smiling broadly, and waved wildly again.

Once more, The Skipper sounded her horn.

Chapter 6

Johnny turned to his mother and asked, "Can we go see Hank?"

"Johnny, he has his work that he has to do. They have gotten in so late. They still have to take care of all the fish that they have caught, and it is almost dark already."

"Oh, please?" Johnny pleaded.

"Not today. Besides, we came here to see the sunset."

"Pretty, please, can't we just go see him for just a few minutes?"

"No, Johnny, we don't want to make pests of ourselves. Now come on, let's go back over to the beach and watch the sunset from there."

"Okay," Johnny said reluctantly, and followed her back over to the beach.

By the time they sat down together upon the sand, the horizon was already starting to turn mauve and golden. Then the sun kissed the lip of the ocean and she dazzled. Her white caps turned into pink cotton candy and some of the rolling waves to molten gold. The clouds above the sun turned apricot. The sun dipped into the water and the water on the horizon blazed like red lava, and the clouds that just had been apricot turned deep orange.

"This is so beautiful," Lilly said, as she put her arm over Johnny's shoulders and pulled him closer to her.

"It sure is," Johnny said in agreement. "It looks a lot different than it did last night, doesn't it?"

"It certainly does."

Johnny asked, "Do you think it will look different tomorrow night?"

"I don't know. We'll just have to wait and see."

"Do you mean that we can come down here again tomorrow night?"

"I don't see why not?" Lilly answered.

"Gee, that would be just swell, Mom."

She looked down at him in the diminished light and smiled. "I thought that you might like that."

He slipped his arms around her waist and squeezed. "I love you, Mom. You're the best."

She kissed the top of his head and said, "I love you too, Johnny."

"I'm hungry!" he said

"I am too. Let's go back and have some dinner." She stood up and brushed off the sand, pulled Johnny to his feet and turned to head back to her car, just as the sports car pulled away. This night they had not been alone, yet again.

By the time they returned to the lodge, it was very chilly. The wind whipped the skirt of her dress about her legs when she stepped out of her car in front of the lodge. Johnny ran ahead of her and held the huge door open for her, proudly. "What a little gentleman you are," she said to him, as she passed by him and stepped inside the lodge. Johnny's face lit up with pride. He scurried around her and held open the swinging door to the kitchen.

The evening cook approached the two of them and extended a plump hand to Lilly. "Hello," he said, "you must be the new morning cook."

She took his hand and shook it. "Yes," she said, "I'm Lilly and this is my son Johnny."

"Well, I'm Howard and I believe I cooked your meal last evening."

C. S. Crook

"You, Howard, are an excellent cook. I can only dream of being able to cook like that. The meal last night was amazing."

Johnny piped up and said, "I liked it too. Can you teach my mommy to make meatballs like that?"

Both adults laughed and Howard said, "Well, Johnny, that would be my pleasure."

"Would you have a recommendation for our meal this evening, sir?" Lilly asked.

"Please, call me Howard."

"Yes, Howard," Lilly said softly, almost shyly.

"For Johnny, I recommend the raviolis. I think they are even better than the meatballs."

"Wow, then I have to have them!" Johnny said enthusiastically.

Howard smiled broadly and then turned to regard Lilly. "And for you, my dear, may I recommend the Crab Louie. I know that the ladies around this town are crazy for it."

"Then, Crab Louie it is," she smiled warmly up at him. "Who am I to second guess all the ladies of the town?"

"Trust me, they have nothing on you," he said to her and winked.

Lilly blushed and said, "We had best leave you to your work."

"I will have your order ready in no time," he said, smiling good naturedly.

Lilly escorted Johnny to the employee table at the back of the kitchen. Shortly thereafter, Rudy appeared from around the corner. His hazel eyes lit up and sparkled as soon as he saw them at the table. "Howard told me that I could find the two of you back here. How was your first day?" The question was meant for Lilly, but Johnny thought it was a general question that he was delighted to answer. "I made lots of friends today."

"You did?" Rudy raised his eyebrows, in mock surprise.

"I surely did. I found other kids to play with and met Mr. Trouble and his dog. They are all my friends now."

"I'll bet you make friends everywhere you go?" Rudy said.

Johnny shrugged and said, "Yeah, pretty much." Rudy looked at Lilly, quizzically.

"Today was lovely. It was a lot of hard work and a lot to learn, and more tomorrow. But, I've never been one to be afraid of hard work, and Gus was a joy to work with."

"Well, it sounds like it is going to be a good fit for all of us. It is chilly out, and I thought that perhaps I might be able to get you two some warm chocolate?"

Johnny smiled and Lilly nodded and said, "That is so kind of you, Rudy, thank you."

He waved it off and said, "I'll be back in a flash." He curtly spun on his heel and was gone.

"I like Rudy," Johnny said to his mother.

Lilly smiled at him and said, "Me too." Then, she frowned a little and asked, "Who is this new friend of yours, Mr. Trouble?"

"Oh, I was meaning to tell you all about him over lunch, but you had to work and then I was so excited that I had met the other kids, I just plumb forgot to tell you."

"Well, I'm all ears now."

Howard rounded the bank of ovens, with a plate in each hand. "Here you two are. Ladies are always first," he said, and set a salad piled high upon a plate down in front of Lilly. Then he added, "And gentlemen last, but not least." He set a steaming plate of raviolis with white sauce down in front of Johnny.

"This looks absolutely amazing," Lilly said, in obvious appreciation.

"Our goal here is to always amaze," he chuckled. "Enjoy!"

"Thank you," Johnny said.

"You are quite welcome, young man."

"Yes, thank you so much," Lilly said.

"My pleasure, I assure you. Now, if you will forgive me, my duties call."

"Of course, we just want you to know that we are very grateful," Lilly said.

"Those are kind words, thank you," he said, and turned back towards the kitchen.

"You were about to tell me about Mr. Trouble?"

"Hum?" Johnny asked, through a mouth full of raviolis.

Lilly giggled at the sight of him and said, "Oh, I suppose that it can wait." Rudy brought them two mugs of steaming hot chocolate and a bowl of whipped cream. They both thanked him and he returned to his work. Lilly thoroughly enjoyed her salad. She thought to herself that the women of this town were very smart when it came to food. It was the first time in her life that she had ever had crab and she loved it.

"How are your raviolis?" she asked Johnny, just to make small talk, because it was obvious that he was really enjoying them.

"They are so good, do you want a taste?" He held one up on his fork for her to sample. She leaned over the table and took it off his fork with her lips.

Just then, Lou rounded the corner and he was touched by the sight of the little boy feeding his mother. It took him off his guard for a moment. He felt that he had intruded upon something that was personal and special. It was such a tender moment. He started to turn to retrace his own steps. This feeling of the need to retreat was so alien to him.

Johnny looked over at him and called out just then, "Mr. Lou!"

It's too late, Lou thought to himself. He smiled and walked toward the table, "I'm sorry to intrude upon your dinner."

"It is no intrusion, I can assure you. We were just finishing up," Lilly said.

"I just wanted to let you know all the staff that you worked with today said that you met and exceeded all expectations."

Lilly looked surprised for a moment and then gathered her composure. "That is most kind of them," she replied.

He looked sternly at her and said, in his most authoritative voice he could muster at the moment, "They are a hard lot to please."

"Well then, that is even kinder of them to say so. I know that I have much to learn and I'm most eager and honored to learn under such accomplished chefs and staff."

"I think you are off to an excellent start. I also think, if you keep up the stamina and tenacity that you displayed today, you will almost be home free. We will be still looking to draw in some of the southern customers, of course"

"Yes, I understand, and I just want to say, thank you for this opportunity."

"You are welcome. I will leave you now to enjoy the rest of your meal." Lou turned, and walked away.

Shortly, Rudy appeared and said, "Lou thought that the two of you might be ready for dessert?"

"Oh, none for me, I positively couldn't, I am so full."

"I positively could," Johnny replied. Both Rudy and Lilly laughed.

"Do you have some more of that chocolate cake left?" Johnny asked.

"We do have the cake. We bake it fresh every day, but have you tried the cheesecake yet? I highly recommend that as well."

"I have never heard of cheesecake," Johnny said.

"Well, that is even more reason to try it. That's just my humble opinion," Rudy said, encouraging him.

"Okay, you win," Johnny said, and shot him a huge smile. Johnny's smile was infectious and Rudy felt his face mirroring Johnny's.

"Would you care for a cup of coffee, Lilly?"

"I'm fine, Rudy, thank you. I'm afraid that if I had coffee after the hot chocolate, I would be no good for work tomorrow."

"Alright, I will bring one slice of cheesecake and one glass of milk for Johnny."

After Rudy left them to get the cheesecake, Lilly leaned toward Johnny and said, "Johnny, please tell me more about this Mr. Trouble?"

"Well, he is very old and very smart, and he is very sly, like a fox."

"Sly, like a fox, you say. In what way is he sly?" Now, Lilly's curiosity was peaked.

Johnny said, "Just for example, he will pretend like he is really mean and grumpy. I think it is just to see if you scare easily, but if you tough it out and stick around long enough, you will see that he is a really nice man." Johnny fished around in his pocket and pulled out the stinky seed pod and the slightly squished red and yellow berries. "Look, I found these today and I brought them back to ask Mr. Trouble what they are. He will know for sure. This red one here is really sweet, but the yellow one is just okay."

Lilly's face lost its color. "Johnny, you know that you should never eat anything when you're not sure what it is."

He said, "They are both berries."

"Yes, that is true, but some types of berries can be poisonous."

"Oh, I didn't know about that."

"How many did you eat?"

"I ate only one of each."

"Well, you seem to be alright. Johnny, will you promise me that you will not eat anything that you find, without showing it to me first?"

"Yes Mommy, I promise that I will show you first."

"What about that one?" Lilly asked, pointing to the one pod amongst the two berries in Johnny's small open palm. "You didn't eat one of those did you?"

"No, this one is from those tall trees at the edge of the meadow." Johnny plucked the pod from his palm with the fingers of his other hand and said, "Here, smell." Lilly took it from his out stretched hand and sniffed. She immediately crinkled her nose in disgust. "It stinks," he said.

Lilly waved her other hand under her face to clear the air, "Thank you for the warning."

Johnny looked at her with a puzzled look, "What warning?"

"Oh, nothing, it's just a figure of speech, that is all," she said, and handed the pod back to Johnny.

Rudy brought Johnny's cheesecake and set it down in front of him, along with the tall glass of milk. Rudy then placed a fork in front of Johnny and one in front of Lilly as well. He smiled and said, "That is just in case."

She smiled up at his young, freckled face and said, "I'm afraid I'm going to gain some weight here."

C. S. Crook

"I think you have some room to grow," he blushed, and then he quickly added, "That was meant as a compliment, only."

"As a compliment, it was taken, thank you." Still blushing, Rudy hurried away.

Johnny had half of the cheesecake gone, by the time Lilly looked away from the fleeing waiter and back across the table at her son. "I take it that is a wonderful dessert."

Johnny nodded and ran his tongue across his lips. He pushed the plate toward her. "Have a taste, Mommy. It is out of this world."

"Well, with a recommendation like that, I have to at least have a taste." She picked up her fork and took off a small corner of the cheesecake. It was surprisingly good. She nodded her head and said, "Now, that is delicious!"

He said, "See, what did I tell you?"

"I'm starting to learn that you know a thing or two about desserts."

Johnny smiled and said, "Rudy is a big help."

"Yes, he is," she agreed. Lilly watched Johnny as he cleaned up his dessert. She was exhausted and more than ready to turn in for the evening. The moment that he finished, Lilly asked, "Are you ready to go, sport?"

He nodded and slipped down from his chair. Together, they walked out into the chilly night to the car. When Lilly slipped in behind the wheel, she shivered. It was no warmer inside the vehicle. The damp air seemed to engulf and permeate everything in its path, including her weary bones. She cranked the engine to life and turned on the headlights. The Ford rolled out of its parking slot and turned toward the little country lane. The fog lay in a bank in front of the car, and only parted when sliced by the chrome bumper. The fog was so dense that Lilly had trouble seeing the tiny porch light on the cottages. "Wow, this is some scary stuff," she said.

"What is scary?" Johnny asked, with concern clearly in his voice.

"This fog, because it is so hard to see where you are going," Lilly said, while straining to see into the dense grey shroud that seemed to engulf them. She leaned forward over the steering wheel and followed her headlights, cautiously. She thanked God that they didn't have far to go. When the car rolled up in front of their cabin, she turned off the engine and let out a long sigh of relief. They went inside and got themselves ready for bed. Both fell into a much needed deep sleep, almost as soon as their heads hit the pillow.

Chapter 7

The next morning, Lilly had to report to work by 4:30 a.m. She was starting her regular schedule. She got herself ready as quietly as she could and slipped out the door. The fog was gone, but it was still very chilly. She zipped up her coat to her chin, tucked her hands into its deep pockets and walked out onto the lane toward the lodge. She was almost all the way to the lodge, when she heard a vehicle on the lane behind her. She stepped off to the shoulder of the lane to allow it more room to pass by her. Instead, it pulled up beside her and braked to a halt. Surprised, she stopped walking and turned to look at the vehicle. Hank was sitting with his window rolled down and smiling broadly at her. "Well, it looks like I need to drive around in the dark more often. There is no telling what I might find. This is almost enough to make a land lover out of me."

She flashed him a smile and said, "I see that you managed to find me."

"Oh, no little lady, you have it all wrong. You have managed to find me again, that is, away from The Skipper."

"Is that so? You are the one that just showed up just now."

"The Shoreline is my largest customer. They get the first pick of all my prime catch. I've been selling to them for years. So, who is the one that just showed up?"

"Okay, I'll give you that one," she conceded.

"Are you staying here? And what on earth are you doing out here in the dark at this hour?" he asked her.

"I'm going to work."

"You're going to work? You work here at the lodge?"

"Yes."

"What is your job here?"

"I'm a breakfast cook."

"That is a shame."

"Excuse me?" she said.

"No, don't take that wrong. I was just thinking out loud that it is a shame that I'm always on The Skipper when everybody in this town is having breakfast. I would love to try your cooking."

"Working here, I will be getting better at it every day."

"They are training you?" She looked at him and nodded. "That does not sound like the Lou I know. Not even a pretty face like yours is usually enough to crack the hard shell of that old crab. He is a great guy, but a shrewd business man. With that guy, friendship and business never cross paths," Hank said.

Lilly shrugged her shoulders. "I don't know what to tell you, but all I know is that God has blessed me and my little boy. I wish we had more time to chat, but I need to report for work."

"Of course, I didn't mean to detain you."

"No harm was done. I enjoyed chatting with you," she said, and walked across his headlights and up to the path that led into the lodge. Hank took his truck to the loading ramp at the far side of the building.

That morning after Johnny had his breakfast at the lodge he said, "Mommy, could you find me a really big piece of cardboard?"

"I'll find out what I can do." She roughed up his hair affectionately and went back to work.

Curious, Molly asked, "What are you wanting the cardboard for, lad?"

"I'm going to turn it into a sled."

"A sled you say? We have no snow here."

"There is this really huge grassy hill, just beyond the tall trees at the back of the meadow. You see, it's going to be a sled for the grass. I met these other kids about my age and that is what they do most of the time, so they tell me. We all take turns riding our sleds down the slope"

"Just as soon as I get done with this chore, I will put my hands on the perfect sled for you lad."

He beamed at her. "Thank you, Molly, you're swell!" She smiled, and went back to her task at hand. Finally, Molly laid down her knife and said, "Come on, let's go find you that sled." Johnny followed closely behind Molly as she led him out to the loading dock. To the side of the large sliding doors, were mounds of cardboard boxes that had already been broken down. Johnny had never seen so many boxes in one place in his whole life. "Wow, will you look at all those, Molly!"

"There are a lot of them, lad, that is for sure." She walked over to the huge stack, carefully made her selection and pulled it from the pile. "What do you think of this one?"

"I think it is a beauty!"

"When you wear this one out, and that I'm sure you will, there will be plenty more." She handed him the cardboard.

"Gee, thanks, Molly."

"Don't mention it, lad, it is my pleasure."

Johnny took his prize and walked back to the front of the kitchen. "See Mom, isn't this the best?"

"It is the best," she agreed with him. "Johnny, are you going to go to play with the children now?"

"No, I think it might be too early. I was thinking that I would go after lunch, like I did yesterday. I'm going to go show Mr. Trouble my new sled and ask him about the stuff in my pocket."

"All right, I will see you at twelve. You still have the watch, right?"

Johnny dug into one of his pockets and held up the watch for her to see. "I have it right here."

"Good, then I will see you at lunch."

Johnny left the lodge and lugged the large piece of cardboard with him. It was awkward to carry, so halfway to Mr. Trouble's, he figured it wouldn't hurt for one end to drag a little. After all, he did have an almost unlimited supply.

When he got close to Mr. Trouble's little house, Johnny could see the dog laying in the shade of the tree. When Trouble saw Johnny approaching, he stood up and wagged his tail. Johnny set his cardboard down, walked over, and gave Trouble a good, vigorous ear scratch. "I'm happy to see you too, boy." Trouble licked Johnny on the cheek, as if he understood what Johnny had said.

Johnny walked up to the door of the house and timidly knocked. "Mr. Trouble?" Johnny got no response and decided to try once more. This time he knocked with more courage and called out, "Mr. Trouble?" He finally could hear some mumbling from inside. He could also hear Mr. Trouble shuffling toward the door. The door creaked open and Mr. Trouble peered out. "Oh, it is you. How come that mutt didn't bark? I didn't even know anyone was here. I clearly paid too much money for him. I seem to have picked the only one out of the litter with no sense."

"He didn't bark because he knew it was me," Johnny said, in defense of Trouble.

"Bah, I paid hard earned money for a barkless dog. They told me that he had intelligence bred into him."

"He's supposed to bark even at good guys like me?"

"Yes, how is he supposed to know? He is supposed to be vicious, I told you!"

"A smart dog can tell the difference," Johnny said, once again, in Trouble's defense.

"Bah, I say." Mr. Trouble reached up and took his jacket off a peg on the back of the door. He slipped his frail arms into the sleeves. Buttoning up his jacket, he stepped out onto the ramshackle front porch with Johnny.

"Hey, I met some kids in the woods yesterday."

"Then why are you here, bothering me?"

"I needed to get some information from you, because I know that you are really smart."

"Oh, is that so?"

Johnny dug into one of his pockets. He pulled out the pod and two squished berries. He opened his hand so that Mr. Trouble could see his bounty. "I wanted to know what kind of berries these are. I ate one of each yesterday and I wanted to find out if they are safe to eat?"

"You ate these already and now you want to know if they are safe to eat? Does your brain do a lot of backwards thinking like this? If it does, you just might be touched in the head, boy."

"My mother says that I should always ask her before I eat anything that I find in the woods. But they were berries, so I just thought that they would be alright."

"You listen to your momma. She is right. Some berries can kill you as dead as a doornail. But you got lucky this time. Those are wild raspberries. The red one is sweeter."

"Is it because the yellow raspberry isn't ripe yet?"

"Nope, they are two different types. The red one is just sweeter." Mr. Trouble reached over and picked up the pod and held it up to his nose and breathed in deeply. "This is a eucalyptus seed. It is from the eucalyptus trees out yonder," he said, pointing to the tall trees at the edge of the meadow. "It is really good for your sinuses. It will clear them right up in a jiffy. It is used in medicine, just for that reason."

"It sure does smell."

"You will find that a lot of medicine smells and tastes bad too," Mr. Trouble told him.

"I also saw some funny looking birds. I thought you might know what they are."

"Well, how am I supposed to know what they are, if I don't know what in the Sam Hill they look like?"

"They are funny looking and have a feather sticking straight up off the top of their head."

"Oh, those would be quail. Did you see any chicks?"

"No."

"The next time you see one, look closely in the grass behind the momma bird. Usually, there will be a whole group of little chicks, if it is the right time of the year. I've heard that they are good eating, but they are too small for me to bother with."

"Folks eat the chicks?"

"No, they eat the adults. Why would anybody waste their time with the chicks?"

"But, you said the baby chicks."

"Boy, I know what I said. I don't need some half pint a fraction of my age to tell me what I said."

Johnny simply shrugged his shoulders and let it go. "I also saw these real pretty purple flowers. I was going to pick some for my momma, but I forgot."

"If you're already forgetting things at your age, you're really going to be in trouble when you get to be my age."

"I'm going to be sure to remember today. She will be really surprised. Do you know what they are called?"

"This time of the year, they would probably be wild iris."

"Oh, that is right. We saw some on the way into town, when we first got here. That is what mommy called them."

Johnny walked over to his cardboard, picked it up and proudly said, "Look at this beauty! I'm going to make a sled out of it."

"Did your momma drop you on your head when you were a baby?"

"I know, you are thinking of a snow sled, but this is going to be a grass sled. There is this huge grassy hill and all of the kids slide down it on their cardboard."

"Well, if it keeps you out of my hair. Now look, you are just plumb tuckering me out with all your questions. I feel like I need a nap."

"It's not even lunch time yet."

"I'm an early riser, and I can nap anytime of the day I want to!"

"Okay, I will see you tomorrow then."

"I can only hope so."

Johnny took his cardboard back to his cabin and leaned it up against the wall on the tiny porch. He headed toward the meadow. He was anxious to see if he could spot any quail chicks. Once in the meadow, he stepped off the path. He knew that he would have to flush them out, if he wanted to see any chicks. The grass was almost up to his knees. It was still wet with the morning dew, from the heavy fog no doubt, he thought. It didn't take long for the legs of his overalls to become soaked from it. He knew that his mother would be worried about him catching a cold because of it. Women just worry too much, he thought, with a slight smile.

Johnny searched and searched, but he didn't even see an adult quail. Disappointed, he stepped back on the trail and headed toward the eucalyptus trees. Then, Johnny walked beyond the trees and deeper into the woods and, at last, he saw the wild flowers. He stooped down and picked as many of the iris as he could find in that location. He studied the small bouquet in his hand and smiled, because Johnny knew that his mother would be pleased, so he turned and headed back toward the lodge. He could feel his tummy alerting him to the fact that it was nearly noon. Johnny was just wondering what his mother would be serving him for lunch when, from out of a bush, in a flash, a mother quail followed by a whole string of chicks ran up the path ahead of him. They were so cute, Johnny wished he could catch one, but knew he would have to be as quick as a cat to do so. He gave up on the thought just as quickly as it entered his mind. His tummy growled and his thoughts about lunch resumed.

At the lodge, the seagulls were there sitting upon the ropes and were looking at him expectantly. One of the larger ones turned its head sideways and squawked at him loudly. "Alright, I will remember to bring all of you something from my lunch today."

Johnny pushed open one of the large doors, being careful not to damage the delicate flowers that he held in his hand. Jo Lynn was standing at her station near the front entrance, saw the flowers in his hand and smiled widely. She escorted him to the swinging set of doors and announced with mock formality, "Miss Lilly, you have a very handsome suitor."

Lilly looked up from her work and saw little Johnny standing there with flowers in his hand and wet legs from the knees down. He flashed a winning smile and proudly held the flowers up for her. Her heart melted. She set down the spatula that was in her hand and walked over to him and gave him a hug and a kiss on the cheek. "You are very thoughtful, Johnny. These are very lovely, where did you find them?"

"I found them just beyond the eucalyptus trees." Then, he added excitedly, "I saw some quail chicks. They were so tiny and as cute as can be."

His stomach growled loudly and Lilly laughed. "It looks like you worked up an appetite."

"I sure did. I'm practically starving."

"I don't see how. Not after that huge breakfast that you had this morning. Go ahead and go sit down and I will get something for you."

Johnny walked to the back and Molly was nowhere to be seen. He sat down and waited for his lunch.

Shortly, his mother brought him a huge bowl of steaming vegetable soup and half a meatloaf sandwich. "Here, maybe this will keep you from catching a cold. Your legs are soaking wet."

"Oh Mom, they will dry in no time. After lunch, I'm going to go sledding with the other kids and it will be sunny on the hill." He dipped his spoon into his soup and paused, holding the spoon just in front of his lips. "Can I have some of those little round crackers that I had yesterday?"

"Sure, I will get you some." Lilly left and came back moments later with his crackers and a glass of milk for him.

"Where is Molly?" he asked.

"Lou sent her on an errand into town. She will be back soon."

"Oh, I see," Johnny replied.

"I must get back to work." She leaned down and gave him another kiss on the cheek.

"What's that for?" Johnny asked.

"That is for the lovely flowers that you picked for me." She turned and headed back to the front of the kitchen.

As soon as she was out of sight, Johnny emptied the small bowl of oyster crackers into one of the pockets of his overalls. He knew that his mother would disapprove, because she would think that it was wasteful feeding the seagulls, but he had promised them twice now. This time, he intended to make good on that promise because, after all, he was a man of his word. He finished his lunch and headed toward the swinging doors on his way out.

"Johnny, I will be off work at three o'clock today."

He took the watch out of one of his pockets and walked it over to her. She knelt down and said to him, "The big hand will be here on the twelve, the same as before, but for three o'clock the little hand will be on the three, right here."

He nodded his head indicating that he understood. "I will be back at the cabin at three o'clock."

"Good, I will see you then. Have fun with the other children."

Johnny walked out of the lodge and up the lane to get his cardboard. He could hardly wait to try it out, so he quickened his pace. Johnny got his cardboard and half carried it and half dragged it along beside him. He followed the path that he had taken the day before, trying to hold his breath past the skunk cabbage, but there were just so many of them scattered about. Finally, he drew near the hill and even before he could see them he knew the children were there, because he could hear their squeals of joy.

Chapter 8

When he came within sight of the other children he waved to them. Hazel was sitting on her sled and just getting ready to make her descent, so she was the first to see him. She smiled a dazzling smile and waved with huge, swiping arcs of her arm. Then, she launched off the top of the hill on her sled and was headed right for him. Her red ringlets were flying and bouncing behind her and her cheeks were rosy against her creamy skin. She had him so mesmerized that he was nearly caught off guard. This was the second day in a row that he had to dodge an incoming sled.

Hazel looked up at him with her dark green eyes and flashed him another smile. "I nearly took you out!"

Johnny had to think quickly on his feet. The last thing he wanted to do was look silly in front of her. He replied, "You did not, no way. I was playing chicken with you."

She stood up, picked up her sled and started back up the hill. "Well then, you must be the chicken, because you are the one that jumped out of the way." That plan had clearly backfired on Johnny. He was trying to think of a way to recover, when she turned and asked him, "You're coming aren't you?"

"Sure, I'm coming; my plan is to try to wear this sled out today."

Hazel replied, "That looks like some pretty sturdy cardboard, if you ask me."

"Well, I can always try."

"You can try."

While they were on their way up the hill, Fred went flying past them. He was laughing and whooping all the way down. Bobby was poised on his sled, waiting for Fred to safely clear the way, before he launched. Bobby waved and called out to Johnny, "Hey, Johnny, I'm glad you could come and play today."

Johnny waved and smiled warmly at Bobby. "I could barely wait to come back here." Bobby nodded and then he was off, down the hill. He was laughing and whooping like his big brother.

When they reached the top of the hill, Johnny started to get in the line behind Hazel. She stepped aside and said, "I just got to have a turn and you have not had one yet, why don't you go in front of me?"

"That's awfully nice of you, Hazel," Johnny said, just a little bit surprised by her offer.

"That gives you a head start on wearing that out today," she said, and grinned at him.

Johnny blushed a bit. "Thank you," he said, and stepped up in front of her.

"How come you're letting him cut in line, Hazel?" Leslie demanded to know.

"He hasn't gotten to have a turn yet today," Hazel responded.

"You wouldn't let either one of us cut in front of you, would she, Lester?" All eyes turned and looked at Lester, as he tried to look stern and shook his head no.

"He isn't cutting in front of either one of you now, is he?" Hazel replied, sounding only slightly irritated.

Fred walked up at the tail end of the confrontation and asked, "What's going on?"

To Johnny's surprise, Donna stepped out of line from her position near the front and announced, "Leslie is being a busybody again." Leslie glared at Donna and Donna popped back into the line.

"So what's new?" Fred asked nonchalantly and stepped into the line behind Hazel, and some of the children giggled.

72

"Humph!" Leslie snorted, and flounced back around and faced the front of the line.

Johnny felt a bit uncomfortable for a few moments, but the children resumed their play as if nothing had transpired, so he too relaxed and soon forgot about it altogether.

His sled turned out to be perfect. It was fast and sleek, all the qualities of a good sled. The children played on the hill for the better part of an hour, when Bobby said, "Hey, what do all of you say that we show Johnny the beach?"

Hazel turned to Johnny and said, "It is really neat there. I think you will like it."

"I like the beach. You guys have one down here?" he asked her.

"Come on, follow us, we will show you," Bobby said, and turned to lead the way. The children all left their cardboard at the top of the hill and followed Bobby. Bobby led them down to the small creek and they followed it, as it meandered through the little valley full of skunk cabbage and the big green leafy plants. The dirt was turning from loam into a sandy loam, and then to sand beneath their feet. The huge clumps of tall grass with the feathers that towered over their heads became more frequent. The roar of the ocean was now echoing throughout the small valley. Johnny was becoming increasingly more excited. He loved to explore more than anything else. They followed the creek around a slight bend and there, spread before him, was a small beach and the Pacific Ocean stretched for as far as his eyes could see. His heart was pounding in his chest. The air seemed electrified with excitement. All the children broke into a run towards the crashing waves.

They stopped just short of the waves, only long enough to yank their shoes and socks off from their feet. They flocked into the water, splashing about and running along the shoreline, chasing each other. They grew tired of that game and then chased the receding waves, only to run from the incoming breakers, squealing and shouting with sheer joy. Finally, exhausted, the entire lot of them collapsed upon the sand, grinning ear to ear and panting like a group of puppies.

Johnny dug his feet into the sand and relished in its warmth. He looked over at Hazel next to him and she was looking at him. She blushed and quickly looked away. He had that funny feeling again, he couldn't understand it. It never happened when he looked at Leslie or Donna. Perplexed, he simply shook his head.

Bobby dug his feet into the sand and used his hands to cover his legs with the sand. Soon, all the children were doing the same thing.

"Do you guys come down here to play often?" Johnny asked the group.

Fred answered his question. "Only on the days that it is sunny and warm, otherwise, it is just too cold. After you get wet, you are freezing." Some of the others nodded in agreement.

"The sand helps warm us up," Donna said.

"Wow! That is the second time you have said something in one day, Donna," Johnny said in mock surprise.

She blushed and clammed up. The children watched the waves roll in and a pelican made an appearance and dropped from the sky in a nosedive, straight into the ocean. "Wow, will you look at that!" Johnny exclaimed. Then, he couldn't believe his eyes when it emerged from the water with a huge fish tail flapping out from the side of its beak. "That is so neat!" Johnny said. The other children looked unfazed by it.

Fred replied to Johnny, "Those pelicans do that all the time."

"Did you see how big that fish was?" Johnny said, excitedly.

Fred merely nodded his head. Shortly, he said, "We had better get back."

The children all stood up and brushed the sand off their wet legs, the best that they could. They sat back down upon the sand and put their socks and shoes back on. This time, Bobby led the way back up the creek into the valley. Along the way, Johnny saw a skunk cabbage and asked the others, "What is the stinky plant?"

74

"That is a skunk cabbage," Hazel said, "we have a lot of them around here."

Lester chimed in, "And we have a lot of skunks too!" Wow! Johnny thought to himself, Lester can speak.

Fred added, "You hardly ever see them during the day, but at night they are everywhere."

"If you toss out marshmallows, you are almost certain to see one. They love marshmallows," Hazel said, and smiled sweetly.

"We have lots of raccoons too," Leslie told him. "You'll also see them mostly at night. They like garbage cans."

Fred said, "Yeah, I always have to clean up after their mess at my house. My dad always threatens to shoot them, but Mom won't let him, she thinks they are too cute."

"They are cute," Johnny agreed.

Fred countered that remark. "Well, you wouldn't think so, if you had to clean up after them as many times in a week that I have to."

"Maybe then, I would change my mind," Johnny conceded.

Bobby turned and looked back at Johnny and said, "Some morning, if we can make it down here early enough, before the tide comes in, we can show you the tide pools."

"What is a tide pool?" Johnny asked.

"They are really neat," Bobby replied, and all the children nodded in agreement. He added, "They are little pools of water left on the rocks when the tide goes out. And sometimes, if you are really lucky, there will be little crabs and sea urchins and stuff like that trapped in the pools."

"What is a sea urchin?" Johnny wanted to know.

"It is hard to explain what they look like. You will have to wait until we can show you one. Of course, they are not always in the tide pools, but sometimes they are," Bobby said.

"Okay," Johnny replied.

"Hey, Johnny, check this out," Fred called out. Fred was bending over and pointing at something on the ground.

Johnny walked over to where Fred was standing and looked down at what he was pointing at. "Ugh, that is disgusting looking! What is it?" Johnny wanted to know.

"That is a banana slug!" Fred said, quite pleased with himself that he was able to get that reaction from Johnny. "If we had some salt, we could show you something really neat!"

"It's not neat, it is disgusting, Johnny. It's even more disgusting than what that looks like now," Hazel told him.

Fred said, "Oh, Hazel, that is only because you are a sissy. Any boy would think it was neat."

Leslie piped up and said, "Lester doesn't like it either!"

Fred said, "Well then, what does that make you, Lester?"

"I didn't say that?" Lester came to his own defense.

Leslie retorted, "Uh huh, yes you did. You told me that the last time they put salt on a banana slug." Lester gave her a less than pleased look and didn't say another word.

Now, Johnny's curiosity was piqued. "What happens when you put the salt on it?" he asked anyone that would answer.

Fred was pleased to offer up the information, "It starts to foam and ooze. Then, it gets all bubbly and dies."

"That sounds mean," Johnny said. Hazel smiled and instinctively stepped closer to Johnny.

"Oh, it's just a slug," Fred said. Johnny let the comment go.

76

Bobby turned and resumed his trek into the valley. The others followed, leaving the slug behind. Soon, they reached the hill and gathered up their sleds. Johnny said, "I hope to see all of you tomorrow."

Bobby told him, "We should all be right here; the same place, at the same time."

"Good, then I'll be here too."

Hazel smiled and he smiled back, then he turned and headed home, and the other children left in the opposite direction.

Johnny reached into his pocket to fish out the watch. He had forgotten all about the time. He was just having too much fun. Please don't let it be past three o'clock, he thought to himself. He stopped to look at the small face of the watch. It was almost three o'clock. He stuffed it back into his pocket and broke into a jog. He didn't want to worry his mother again today. He stepped out from under the eucalyptus trees and into the meadow, just as Lilly was leaving the lodge. He scurried toward her, she saw him and waved. Lilly walked up the lane and waited for him at the juncture, where the path met the lane in front of the other cabins. She saw that his overalls were wet from the knees down again, but this time they had sand still clinging to them in some patches.

"What on earth have you been up to?"

"My friends took me to a beach today."

"There is a beach near here?"

"Uh huh, it is a small one; we had a lot of fun there."

"Johnny, you need to be careful and not go into the water past your ankles. You don't know how to swim and I doubt that any of those other children can swim either." She wished that he wouldn't go near the beach at all, but knew that if the other children did, so would he.

"None of us went in above our ankles. The waves were splashing us."

"That is good then. It sounds like your friends may have some good sense."

"Not even Fred went in past his ankles," he assured her.

"Who is Fred?"

"He is the oldest; I think he might be ten years old. He and Bobby are brothers."

They walked together to their cabin. On the way, he told her about the banana slug. She replied, "Honestly, I can say that I'm happy that I missed seeing that."

"Hazel said that she does not like them either."

"Who's Hazel?"

"Oh, she's just a girl," Johnny replied quickly, with a shrug of his shoulders, and Lilly smiled.

Johnny leaned his sled against the cabin and the two of them went inside. Lilly closed the door and said, "Johnny, I hope you don't mind if I lay down for a bit, just to rest my eyes. I got up so early this morning."

"No, Mommy, you go ahead."

"Johnny, you need to get out of those wet overalls and hang them up in the bathroom to dry. You can put on your other pair."

"Okay, I will, Mommy."

Lilly lay down upon her bed and closed her eyes. Johnny went into the bathroom and changed his overalls. By the time that he came out, his mother was sound asleep. He crawled upon the bed and lay down next to her, and snuggled up against her. He also fell asleep, moments later.

Lilly woke up and saw Johnny sleeping soundly next to her. She was surprised that she had fallen asleep. She carefully crawled over Johnny and stood up beside the bed. She looked down at him and her heart welled up with love. She looked over at the clock that sat upon the dresser and was alarmed by the time. She leaned over the bed and shook Johnny softly. "Johnny, wake up!" Johnny didn't stir, so she tried again. "Johnny, you need to wake up or we're going to miss the sunset."

"What?" Johnny asked, rubbing the sleep from his eyes.

"If we don't get going, we are going to miss the sunset. I overslept."

Johnny sprang up off the bed and began pulling on his socks and shoes. "Let's get going, Mommy."

Lilly grabbed the keys and they were off toward the harbor in no time at all. As they passed the boat docks, Johnny pointed and said to his mother, "Look, Mommy, Hank's boat is over there. Can we stop and say hello to him, please?"

Lilly looked over at one of the docks and sure enough, The Skipper was tethered to the dock. The Skipper gently bobbed up and down as the water rolled under her. "No, Johnny, he and Tony have their work to do."

"Ah, Mom, we won't get in their way."

"I'm sorry, he is a nice man, and he will pretend that we are no trouble. He is losing daylight. Now is a bad time." Johnny slid down in his seat. "I know that you are disappointed, but grownups have to make a living." They drove the rest of the way down to the beach and walked up to the water, hand in hand. The sun was sinking low upon the horizon and a chill was starting to fill the night air. Lilly let go of Johnny's hand and kneeled down upon the sand in front of him. "Here, let me button up your coat for you. It is getting cold already." When Lilly finished buttoning his coat, Johnny plopped down upon the sand. Lilly sat down next to Johnny and together they waited for nature's show. The sound of the ocean was almost hypnotic to Johnny. After all, it had been a long day.

Chapter 9

"I hope I'm not crashing the party," a male's voice said, from behind them. Startled, Lilly spun around from her sitting position, upon all fours.

"Mommy, it's Hank!"

"I can see that it is him," she said, with relief in her voice. "You scared me half to death."

He smiled, sheepishly. "I didn't mean to frighten you so. I was just wondering if I may join the two of you land lovers, for a viewing of the sunset from your perspective? Then, I would like to invite both of you to view it from my perspective, on board The Skipper, out in the open water."

Johnny sprang off the sand as quickly as a tightly wound up jack-in-the-box. He was in front of Lilly and shaking her shoulders and pleading with her. "Mommy, can we? Oh, please, can we go? This is the second time that he has mentioned taking us out on The Skipper."

"I think I'm clearly outnumbered here," she said, with a big smile.

"Well good, now that is settled," Hank said, and sat down on the sand next to Lilly. "How does this Sunday work for you two?"

"That will be just fine, Sunday is my day off."

"That will be perfect. Sunday is the only day that I give myself to kick around a bit. Sometimes when the fishing is too good to pass up, I go out then too."

"What time? She asked.

"How does four o'clock work for the two of you?"

"Four o'clock would be just fine," she said.

"Then four o'clock it is." Hank smiled and then followed her gaze with his own out to the sea. The sun was nearly kissing the water and the colors dazzled upon the ocean and were reflected back toward the sky. Hank looked at Lilly and said, "The view is beautiful and the sunset is okay too."

Lilly pretended not to hear the compliment. After the sunset she said, "Well, Johnny, we had best be heading back."

Hank stood up and offered his hand to her. She took it and he pulled her up to her feet. Johnny stood up and craned his neck to look up at Hank. "I just can't wait to go out on The Skipper. I have never been on a boat before."

Hank reached down and roughed up Johnny's hair. "I'm looking forward to it also, Captain."

Johnny looked up at his mother. She said, "We will both look forward to seeing you on Sunday, Hank." Together, the three of them walked up to their respective vehicles and headed to their different destinations.

Once back at the lodge, Johnny and Lilly ordered their dinners from Rudy. Johnny told Rudy all about their encounter with Hank. Rudy raised his eyebrows in genuine surprise, when he found out that the lodge's very own young and handsome fishmonger was taking them out. That expression on Rudy's face did not go unnoticed by Lilly. Now I'm in for it, she thought.

They finished their meal, shared a luscious slice of banana cream pie and then headed back to the cabin. The night air had the same bone chilling quality that was now starting to become familiar to the two of them. Johnny was grateful for the warm covers upon his bed, when he slipped under them that evening.

The following morning, Lilly got ready for work and slipped out the door, without waking Johnny. When Johnny woke up, he got up and pulled a warm sweater over his head and pulled on his overalls. He looked in the mirror and raked his fingers through his hair. He felt there was no need for the comb on that morning. When he stepped out onto the porch, the fog was just starting to lift. It hovered above the meadow like a partially drawn curtain and Johnny could tell that the day was going to be a nice one. He walked to the lodge for his breakfast and, as soon as he opened the door, a wonderful aroma whiffed out at him.

Jo Lynn was there to greet him. "Good morning, young man."

"Good morning, Jo Lynn. What is that wonderful smell?"

"Your mother just pulled some banana nut bread out of the oven. I was just thinking of having some of that on my break this morning."

Johnny told her, "That is what I'm going to have also," and he walked through the swinging doors into the kitchen.

His mother smiled broadly when she saw him. "Good morning, Johnny. Would you like some eggs and banana nut bread for your breakfast?"

"I was just thinking about that. Jo Lynn is going to have some too."

"She is? Well then, I will be sure to save her a nice big slice. Do you want hot chocolate too?" She thought she already knew the answer to that question, but she asked anyway.

"I sure do."

"Then go sit down and I will have it all to you in just a jiffy."

Johnny walked around the bank of ovens and walked over to his table. He was happy to see that Molly was there. He grinned and said, "Top of the morning to you, Miss Molly."

Surprised, she looked up from her big pile of potatoes and chuckled. She said, "Top of the morning to you, Johnny. How did your sled work out yesterday, lad?"

"I think it was the fastest one on the hill," he said proudly.

"Well, I'm glad that it worked out for you."

"I plan to wear it out real soon."

"Is that so?" He shook his head affirmatively. "I will keep my eyes peeled for another sleek, fast one for you, lad."

"Thanks, Molly, you're the best." She smiled and returned to her dicing and slicing.

Lilly brought Johnny's breakfast to him and set it down upon the table. "I hope that you will enjoy this."

"Thank you, Mommy, it looks really good."

She patted the top of his head and left him with his food. He ate with relish, he was really hungry. Finally, he picked up the last crumb of the bread with his fingers and popped it into his mouth. He stood up and said to Molly, "I will see you later."

"Ah, I look forward to it," she replied.

Johnny waved to his mother and Gus as he left the kitchen. Jo Lynn was busy seating customers, when he stepped back out into the morning air. He headed up the lane to go see Mr. Trouble. Johnny could not wait to tell him about Hank's offer to take him and his mother out on The Skipper and he wanted to tell him all about the beach that the other children had taken him to. There was just so much to cover that he was hopeful that it wouldn't tucker Mr. Trouble out before he could share it all with him. Johnny turned off the lane onto Mr. Trouble's little driveway.

Trouble was in his usual place and was happy to see Johnny, but Trouble didn't exhibit the enthusiasm that he normally expressed for Johnny. "Hey, Trouble, what's wrong boy?" Trouble looked at the house anxiously and whimpered. Johnny noticed that Trouble's water bowl had been knocked upside down. Johnny took the bowl over to the water spigot and filled it. He took the bowl back over to Trouble and sat it down. The dog lapped at the water thirstily. Johnny walked up to the porch and knocked on the door, but he got no answer. He knocked again and still there was no answer. He waited a few more moments, shrugged his shoulders and walked back down the steps off the porch. Trouble lunged forward against his chain and barked. Johnny stopped in his tracks, stunned the barkless dog had just barked. Trouble was still straining against his chain and whimpered again. Johnny turned and looked back at the house. Trouble barked again. Concerned, Johnny said, "What are you trying to tell me, boy?" Trouble whimpered anxiously and looked at the house behind Johnny. Johnny turned and retraced his steps back up onto the porch. Johnny knocked on the door again and called out, "Mr. Trouble?" There was still no answer. Johnny could plainly see the old rusty truck sitting beside the house. He called again very loudly, "Mr. Trouble, are you in there?" Still, there was no answer. An uneasy feeling was settling into the pit of his stomach. Johnny balled up his little fist and pounded upon the door and yelled, "Mr. Trouble?" Still, only silence answered, so Johnny turned and leapt off the porch, and dashed down the driveway toward the lane. Trouble was straining against the chain and barking wildly.

Johnny ran for the lodge as quickly as he could make his short little legs go. He couldn't remember it ever being this far away. There it was spread right out before him at the end of the lane, but it just seemed to keep receding. His lungs were on fire in his chest and his heart pounded wildly, but he had to go on. Something was wrong; he knew something was very wrong. Finally, Johnny flung back one of the doors to the lodge and burst past an astonished Jo Lynn. Johnny flew through the swinging doors, almost knocking Molly off her feet.

"Johnny, what on earth has gotten into you?" Lilly asked, alarmed.

Johnny was standing before her, clasping a hand on each of his knees. He was gasping, trying to take in air. He was almost totally out of breath. "Mr. Trouble!" he gasped, "Come quick, Mom!"

Lilly asked, "Something is wrong with Mr. Trouble?" Johnny frantically shook his head in affirmation.

"What is wrong with him?"

"I don't know," Johnny gasped, "hurry, Mommy, please."

Please write a review on Amazon or Goodreads. It will be greatly appreciated.

There are six books in 'Johnny's Adventure' series; #1 'Johnny's Reptile Adventure', #2 'The Skipper's Captain', #3 'The Heroic Dog and Boy', #4 'Finding A Home', #5 'The Magic Wishbone', and #6 'Johnny's Treasure Adventure'.

74062421R00051

Made in the USA
Lexington, KY
13 December 2017